WOLVES QUEEN

THE ROYAL HEIR TRILOGY

JEN L. GREY

CHAPTER ONE

Twelve Years Ago

"We've got to leave now." Kassie pressed the button that opened the garage door as her short black hair bobbed in the back.

"Mommy?" I cried as Mona lifted me in her arms, running toward the black Mercedes.

"I'm right here, honey." Mom ran through the garage door, almost tripping over her long gown as she glanced behind her. "We're going to be okay."

"Get in the damn car." Kassie opened the back door and waved for us to hurry.

Mona slid into the seat and scooted over to the other side of the car. She placed me in the middle seat as Kassie climbed in on the other side. They both pulled out guns.

"Get in the damn car, Serafina," Dad's regal voice yelled as he ran and jumped into the driver seat. It was strange with him wearing his royal cut for him to be so informal. "We've got to get the hell out of here."

"Don't harass me." She slid into the seat, yanking at her

golden gown. "I'm in a freaking gown, for Christ's sake." Her long red hair was pulled into an elegant French twist.

It was my favorite hairstyle of hers because normally I could climb in her lap and play with the ends when she was putting me to bed before having to attend some royal event or party.

As soon as Mom's door shut, Dad pressed the gas pedal hard. "I can't believe Darren would do something like this." He grabbed his cell phone and pressed the button. "Open the gates immediately."

I wanted to ask questions about my uncle—Daddy always taught me to be curious—but right now didn't seem to be the time. In times like these, he said a six-year-old didn't need to understand quite yet. That I should still have some time left as a child before completely training to be Queen.

"He's wanted the crown ever since you were little boys." Mom's jade eyes glowed. "He's not half the leader you are."

"That may be fact, but he doesn't see it that way." The gates were open, and Dad pressed the pedal even farther down.

I turned around and looked at our Southampton home. I'd expected to be there a few more days before heading back to our apartment in New York City. This was our nice getaway place to leave the hectic city behind. Daddy always said that a wolf should spend more time with nature. Our lot was over ten acres with the house surrounded by woods. He and Mom would shift every day and go run for hours. I couldn't wait until I had my first shift and joined them. The years seemed so far away.

"How did you find out about the plans?" Dad glanced in the rearview mirror, focusing on Kassie.

"Well, you know how it was odd that he planned on

coming?" Kassie sighed and shook her head. "He never leaves the city, but he called me when he found out that you were meeting with the heads from the United Kingdom. He said he needed to be there or something dumb may happen."

"Yes, I already know this." Dad punched the steering wheel. He ran his fingers through his short dark hair. "I'm sorry. It's just... he's my brother."

Kassie frowned. "I know, but when I saw him pour the wolfsbane in both yours and Elena's drinks..."

"They were trying to kill my baby too?" Mom turned around and touched my leg. "He's been getting worse and worse over the years. When we had Elena..."

"As King, I should've noticed this before now." He focused his eyes on the road as he took the sharp turns.

"It must be a mistake." My uncle wouldn't try to kill me. He used to give me extravagant presents when he traveled. I still had my favorite kangaroo stuffed animal from Australia. "He gives me presents."

"Oh, baby." Mom's shoulders slumped. "I know."

A car raced up behind and blew its horn.

"What the hell is going on?" Dad turned his head, and his eyes widened with fear. "No, this can't be happening."

The car rammed into the back of us, making me lurch forward and hit the seat. "Ow." Why would that person do that?

Our car skidded into the oncoming lane, but it was dark and thankfully empty. The car behind us sped up and moved into the other lane, driving so fast it was reaching us again.

"Hurry, Corey," Mom yelled as she turned to look at me once more.

I jerked forward, trying to get to her. I needed her. I needed Mommy.

There was a lurch as the car rammed into our side. We fell over on the side Mommy and Mona were sitting on and then began rolling over and over. The front windshield broke and crashed all around us. The front of the car slammed into a tree before we tipped over the side of the road and dropped into water.

My head was dizzy, and my arm hurt. I needed my mommy right now.

"Roll down the window before we can't," Mona yelled as the engine still roared.

"I'm trying." Kassie groaned.

I unbuckled my seatbelt, needing my parents. I needed them to hold me and tell me everything was going to be all right. When I broke free and leaned over the seat. Our car was in the water, floating. "Mommy, I didn't know cars could do this."

When she didn't answer, my heart took off. She always answered me. She told me I was her joy. Something had to be wrong. "Mommy? Daddy?"

"My window is down. Let's get out of here," Mona yelled. "Your highnesses, can you get yours down too?"

Once again, there were no answers.

"No." Kassie grabbed me and shoved me into Mona's arms. "Go now. They'll come back."

"But Mommy. Daddy." I couldn't leave them. She had to be out of her mind.

"Take her now, Mona."

I didn't understand. Kassie was looking strange. She was so pale, which didn't make sense. Wolves in our pack had olive skin.

Mona released me and climbed out of the window. "Here, hand her to me."

"No, Mommy." I tried climbing over the center console, but Kassie yanked me and placed me in Mona's hands.

"Come on, Elena." Mona nodded toward Kassie. "She needs to help your parents."

"Oh, okay." She was going to help them. "Please keep them safe?" My eyes locked onto Kassie's as a tear trailed down her cheek.

A car's doors slammed up above, and Mona placed her hand on my head. "Remember the game you like to play with Daddy in the pool?"

"Yes." I smiled. "Are we doing Marco Polo?"

"Kind of like that, so we need to swim a long way so it's not easy to find us." Mona winked at me, but her smile seemed different.

My spine prickled, but it didn't make any sense. I mean, we were playing a game. Daddy always found me so easily. Maybe this would be the first time that I beat him. "Okay." I smiled as I glanced back at them one more time. "But if they can't find us super-fast, we have to let them know we're okay. They might be scared."

"You've got it." Mona patted my cheek. "On the count of three. One, two, three."

She submerged us in water as the car exploded and everything went dark.

Present Day

My eyes popped open, and I sat straight up in bed. That fucking dream was back. I didn't know why my wolf wanted me to relive that memory over and over. I needed to go visit that witch again, pronto.

I glanced at the clock. Great, six in the morning. I still had an hour before the stupid alarm was supposed to go off. There was no way in hell I was going to try to go back to sleep after that nightmare.

Signs had started to show last week that the magic that hid my wolf was wearing off. I should've gone then, but I had college orientation that felt like it lasted forever, and a group wanted to go out for drinks afterward. So after my classes, my ass would entail going to hunt the witch down. Most of the time, I found her at her store in town, but witches were unpredictable. They usually did as they pleased.

As I scratched my nose, my hand touched wetness on my cheeks. I'd been crying again, just like every other time I had my dream.

My parents died by my uncle's hand. It was still hard to believe after all this time. You'd think that the hurt would ease over time, but it hadn't. Right before I turned sixteen, Mona and Kassie helped me find a witch that would suppress my wolf. At first, they'd been hesitant since I told them I never wanted to be Queen. They put up a fuss. But after I pointed out that if I shifted, my asshole uncle would feel me and know I was alive, they got onboard faster. At that time, we still weren't quite ready for that.

It still rocked me the way wolf hierarchy worked. Since my uncle was considered King, he felt every wolf shifter on North America's continent.

Had they known my other main reason for wanting to keep my wolf contained, they probably wouldn't have helped me. When they realized my true intent, it was too late.

I wanted to be human.

What did being a supernatural get me? Dead parents. I didn't need karma to remind me again of why being human was what I needed to do. If my uncle being a power-hungry asshole wasn't the wakeup call I needed, then I'd have to be an idiot.

That's why today was so important. It was my first official day of being a freshman at the University of South Carolina. It was a decent school and not too crazy-expensive since we lived in town. It would be the first time I wasn't homeschooling in the last several years, which unnerved me. But hell, if I was going to be a human, I had to learn how to be around them.

Forcing myself out of bed, I stood and made myself head over and turn on the lights. It was stupid since I didn't need them, but I had to remember I was human; not half-wolf, so I needed to use them.

I learned early on, if you don't get in the habit of doing things the 'normal' way, then humans looked at you strangely and pulled away. That was what happened at the last place we moved before here. I had just started third grade. I hadn't noticed how different I was until then. I could see so much better than the others and was more connected with nature.

When I'd tell them a storm was coming, they'd laugh. However, it all blew up when I smelled death on the librarian. I had told the teacher and classmates that they needed to say their goodbyes, and they all looked at me strangely. Kassie and Mona got called in as my guardians, and the school told them I needed counseling. When the librarian died two days later, even the teachers were scared to talk to me.

It was as if they thought I caused her death or something. So, it killed my social life, and because of that, we moved away, ending up here. I quickly learned to follow the crowd and not stick out, which was everything opposite of what my parents stood for.

But, at the end of the day, they were dead, and I wasn't, so I figured I should live life by my own rules.

I removed my pajamas and pulled on a snug, black tank top and jeans. I grabbed my hairbrush and looked in the mirror that hung on the back of my closet door. My eyes had dark circles under them, which made my blue eyes stand out more. I was going to have to wear makeup today.

That was one of the worst things about looking in the mirror. I had my father's crystal blue eyes and my mother's long red hair. It was a painful reminder of them.

Not wasting any more time, I grabbed the concealer and rubbed some under my eyes. The last thing I needed was to worry both Kassie and Mona, which would have them making a huge fuss about what was going on. In the past few months, I'd had to go to the witch every other week instead of monthly like I used to do.

They kept telling me that I was an alpha and that if I didn't embrace my wolf, the wolf would take over. I didn't believe them. As long as I went to the witch, I shouldn't have had any major side-effects. I arrogantly pushed this time to three weeks, and I already regretted it. The one nice side-effect of it all was that though other supernaturals couldn't sense me, I could still sense them, especially with my own kind.

After finishing my makeup, I grabbed the brush and ran it through my long red hair. I wore it down all the time. I never wore it up. That's how Mom liked her hair, so I tried to do everything possible to numb the pain.

I tiptoed down the stairs, hoping not to wake the ladies. The past twelve years had brought us closer. They took on raising me, and now they were family. I didn't know where I'd be without them. Probably dead.

"You had that dream again, didn't you?" Mona sat in the den's recliner with a cup of coffee in her hands. Her dark blonde hair was sticking up in various places, and she yawned.

"Uh, no." I hated to lie to them, but they'd only worry more.

She snorted. "I'm not stupid."

"Could you start being just a little bit for me?" The last thing I wanted to do was talk about my feelings and hug it out.

"We raised you well." She lifted her coffee cup in the air in a toast. "But no, you were screaming again. So even if I was stupid, I think I'd figure it out."

"Sorry, I didn't mean to wake you." I pointed at her mug. "You make any more in there?"

"It's a Keurig." Mona arched an eyebrow. "Make it your own damn self."

"I at least had to try." They usually would do stuff like that for me. Yes, I was spoiled. "You know how it is."

"Go get you some caffeine." She waved me away. "I was up extremely late, and I'm so tired I may fall asleep sitting here."

"Now, that's not my fault." She was terribly addicted to Candy Crush. "You just need to remove the app from your phone."

"Hey, I didn't ask to be called out." Mona chuckled and shook her head.

I rolled my eyes at her and walked into the kitchen. I made my way over to the Keurig and hit brew. I grabbed my phone and unlocked it; I had a text in the middle of the night. It was strange that it hadn't woken me.

Hey gorgeous. I can't wait to see you in class today. Hoping we can catch more drinks later. – Connor.

Great, this guy was texting me again. He should've had a clue if he felt compelled to include his name.

There was no telling what he'd say when he saw me again. The last time we saw each other I was drunk and lost my mind. Shifters, in general, have a huge sex drive, and well, he was hot but a clinger. I hated clingers. Now, there was no telling what would happen once I got to school.

CHAPTER TWO

I'd been running the obstacle course at the back of the house, so time flew by. Before I knew it, it was time to head to class.

"Are you running to or from something?" Kassie stepped out onto the back porch and took a sip of the coffee she held in her hand.

"Funny." They weren't completely thrilled with my decision to pretend to be human.

"You're getting faster." Her eyes landed on the course.

Our course had similar items to what a military base had for their cadets that were training. There were several tires lined up that I had to sprint through, a large rope climbing station, a monkey bar station, a net climbing, two tall poles, and a huge wood tower that I had to climb over. And the other half of the yard was a homemade shooting range. "I should be. I've been running it for the past two years." Before that, they had me focus on learning how to fight. Once I had that down, they said I needed to build muscle and learn endurance.

They wanted me battle-trained in case someone ever found us. I didn't mind. It kept me busy, and honestly, I loved that I'd been trained to protect myself. I refused to end up like my parents.

"Very true." She sat in the wooden chair that overlooked the balcony. "I'm going to have to reset some things to make it harder."

"I'm down." I glanced at my watch again and cringed. "Hey, gotta go to my nine o'clock class, and afterward, I'll be hunting the witch down, so don't be surprised if I get home a little later than you expect."

"Fine." She scratched the side of her face, which was her tell. She was contemplating whether she should bring something up or not.

The longer she thought about it, the harder the conversation was going to be. "Spill."

She snorted. "We've trained you too well."

"Hurry, I'm going to be late." The last thing I wanted to do was stay here and hear this again, but it would save me annoyance in the long run.

"You've been going to the witch so often. Are you sure..."

"Don't worry. I don't owe her anything. I bring her herbs and give her a little of my blood, and we're even." She once started telling me why she needed my blood, and I stopped her. I remember saying, "As long as it doesn't impact me, then I didn't give a shit." She seemed to be happy with that answer.

"The blood is what I'm worried about," Kassie huffed.

"I looked it up online." I had told her I didn't want to know, but one night, curiosity got the best of me. "It's for killing vampires." Any way I could help reduce the supernatural population, I was in.

"Well, I can't complain about that." She tilted her head to the side. "But I'm not one hundred percent sure about your reasons."

"I'm eighteen now, so you're kinda stuck dealing with my decisions." I grabbed my purse and keys off the ground. "So we're just going to have to agree to disagree."

"You better be damn glad I love you." Kassie took another long sip. "Hurry up, and don't be late. I'll have us some steaks for dinner tonight."

My stomach growled just at the thought. "Yeah, make sure mine is rare. Last time, you overdid it."

"I got distracted by Aquaman." Kassie pointed her finger at me and arched an eyebrow. "That means it was justified. Besides, I make one mistake, and you won't let me live it down."

"Because it's food." Jason Momoa or not, food should never be ruined. It was a damn travesty. "See ya."

"Be careful." She shouted as I opened the privacy gate and headed to my car.

My car wasn't fancy by any means, but I love my little Honda Civic. It was cute, clean, and best of all, a dark red. I pulled out of the driveway and made my way to class.

―――――――

I PARKED in the general student parking lot, which happened to be at least a mile away from where I needed to be. It was ten minutes until class started, so I had to hurry.

Luckily, it was a beautiful day. The sun was out, and as always, it was burning up in August. That was one of the things I missed about New York. At least in the city, it was only this miserable for five months out of the year instead of eight like here. Usually around October, it finally began cooling off here.

I grabbed my purse and backpack and slammed the door. I took off and hit the lock button as I went.

"Well, hey there." A guy nodded at me as I rushed past him.

Ugh, men are such idiots. Not wanting to waste any of my time, I ignored him and pushed my legs faster.

"Dumb bitch." The guy mumbled under his breath, thinking I couldn't hear him.

But of course, I had exceptional hearing without my wolf. Normally, I'd turn around and tell him where he could go, but I needed to hurry. I tried to stay under the radar, so I didn't want to rush in late.

It was sometimes hard hiding how fast I could be, yet another thing that kept me not human. So I tried moving slower than I wanted.

The brick building appeared, and I rushed up the four steps and straight through the doors. My class was on the first floor, so at least I had that going for me.

Within a minute, I entered the classroom and scanned the open desks. Of course, Connor was in this class, and he waved me over to an open seat next to him.

Oh, hell, no.

My eyes scanned past him, and I spotted an open seat in the very back. That's where I wanted to be. I slipped between a few desks and walked through the aisle, heading for my perfect seat.

"Elena," Connor called as if he thought I hadn't seen him.

That night proved, over and over again, how much of a mistake it'd been. I unzipped my bag and pulled out my book for class.

"I think that guy is hollering for you." A girl leaned over and giggled. "He's pretty hot."

"If you're into the needy kind." I met her gaze and rolled my eyes. "Seriously, he's a clinger."

The girl shrugged, and her hazel eyes twinkled. "Some wouldn't mind a guy looking like that being that way." She tilted her head, causing her blonde hair to cascade over her shoulder.

"From what I gather from you, you wouldn't like him either." She had on a stylish red wrap dress, which made her eyes and hair pop. She was put together, but there was something independent I saw in her eyes.

"You think you already know me?" She laughed and straightened her shoulders.

"No, but it's your body language." I motioned to where we sat. "You're trying to blend in and not stick out. Your dress is trendy; your nails are painted a light pink as if it was planned for the outfit, and you seem put together. Women who are put together don't want someone needy." Or they're emotionally unavailable like me.

"I'm not sure if I'm impressed or horrified that you pegged me so quickly." She glanced at the ceiling and shrugged. "I'll have to get back to you on the verdict."

"Oh, I'm so eager to hear your decision." My words were sarcastic. It wasn't like I cared what she thought anyway.

"Hey, now." She glanced at me. "Do you know who I am?"

And here, I thought she wouldn't get on my nerves. Boy, was I wrong. "No, and frankly, I don't give a rat's ass. I'm here to learn and leave."

An older man entered the classroom with gray hair and

glasses. He glanced at the class and smiled. "Hi. I'm Professor Smith, so let's get started."

As soon as the clock turned to nine-fifty, I stood from my seat and headed to the door.

"Hey, I wasn't quite done yet." The professor's eyes widened when they landed on mine.

"Well, times up, and I've gotta go." Just because he was a teacher didn't mean shit to me when it came to them running over, and honestly, Connor had eyed me several times throughout the class, and I didn't want to deal with him. "See ya Wednesday." I turned and walked out of the class with a few students snickering behind me. I wanted to visit the witch before my next class started.

It only took a few minutes for me to make my way back to my car and get moving. I needed to get to the store and fast. I just hoped she got there on time. Sometimes she ran late, but I'd wait. At least there was a Qdoba nearby if I needed to grab something to eat. My stomach grumbled at the thought.

The storefront wasn't too far from campus, so I rolled into the parking lot ten minutes after ten. I turned the car off and climbed out, heading straight to the door. I scanned the window for the open sign, and my heart skipped a beat when I saw the sign was lit.

At least that was one win for the day. I quickly opened the store's door and stepped into the dark room.

This place always gave me the willies. The overpowering stench of rosemary always made me want to gag. I passed the rows of bowls, herbs, and cards to head straight to the counter.

"I dreamed about you last night." Rose appeared from the back room. Her long black hair waved down her back, and her amber eyes were mesmerizing. She had to be only a couple of years older than me, but you could never be sure. Witches could glamour themselves and appear to people however they wanted. To see a witch's true face was rare, and only those as close to her as her coven were the ones who received such honor. For all I knew, she could have gray hair and be hunched over. "Something happened last night to weaken the magic."

Yeah, reliving my parents' death was a doozy. "So you knew I'd be here today."

"Of course." Her red lips spread into a big smile. "The usual payment if you don't mind."

"Fine." I held my hand out on the counter. "I forgot the herbs this time."

She laughed again. "No worries. The blood is what I need most. We have vampires sniffing around our coven."

That was the most information she'd given me before. "That sucks. Good luck with that."

"You're one interesting girl." She pulled a knife from her black dress pocket and held it above my hand. "I can feel the strength and will inside you. Why do you keep wanting to hide it?"

"If you're going to ask questions, I'll find someone else." She handled the exchange as a mutually beneficial arrangement. Now, she was getting nosey, which wasn't part of the deal. And witches were the worst gossipers of every supernatural race.

"Fine." She huffed and held my pointer finger with her left hand. "No need to get all grumpy." As she inserted the dagger into my skin, a drop of blood puddled on the tip of my finger.

The metallic scent swirled in the air, but that was par for the course.

She released my hand and grabbed a small bottle. "Pour some in here." She twisted the lid off and handed the glass container to me.

"Yeah, I know." I squeezed my pointer finger, making sure several large drops coated the bottom. "Here you go."

"Good girl." She chuckled as she took the bottle and placed the lid back on.

"No dog jokes." I wasn't sure how comfortable I was with her changed attitude. "Now, let's do this. I'm hungry."

"Ahhh..." Rose pointed at me and nodded. "That's what your problem is today. Next time, eat before you get here. It's hard enough to handle you when you aren't hangry."

I kept coming back here due to her blunt nature. We knew exactly what side we stood on. "Yeah, yeah. Just do it."

"Fine." She grabbed some herbs and crushed them in her hands. She mouthed some words silently and placed the herbs in my hand. "There. Done."

I'd always wondered what she said for the spell, but she told me only coven members are allowed to hear one another's spells. Something about trade secrets or some shit like that.

As the magic settled in me, my wolf began to retreat back into her cage. She hated it, but this was the best for both of us. If we were meant to be rulers, fate wouldn't have intervened.

"You need to be careful." Something flashed in her eyes. "Were you around anyone today? You have a wolf scent on your skin."

"What? No." In all transparency, I made myself not scan for other supernaturals. The more you were attuned to the world, the more you became a target. "At least, I don't think so."

"If you're beginning to make contact with new wolves other than your two caretakers, it's going to make the magic wear off faster, so you'd better be careful. Your wolf grew beside those two and doesn't feel threatened." She grabbed a pink sticky note and wrote down her name and number. "Look, we've been doing these charades ever since you were a little girl. I don't want to see something bad happen to you, so take my number. Call me if you need me, no matter the time."

"So what will this cost me?" With witches, you had to be careful. They were sneaky as fuck and strong as hell.

"A future favor." She crossed her arms and stared me down. "I've always been able to see glimpses of people's futures. Even yours. But now when I look at you, all I see is black."

"Huh." Black wasn't usually a good color when tied to magic. "Maybe I've escaped death once, and it's coming back around for me." I should've died that day with my parents. It seemed wrong to live. They died way too soon. The world still needed them. Hell, I still needed them.

"No, it's not that." She tilted her head and crossed her arms. "It's that your future isn't set in stone yet. You're about to come to a crossroads. One where a choice has to be made."

"Let's be clear." She was giving me the heebie-jeebies. "My future is set, and there won't be any changing it." Kassie or Mona must have come by here and said something to her. "Thanks for this." I grabbed the sticky note and put it in my jeans pocket. I wasn't about to turn down an offer like that. Next time I needed her and she wasn't at the store, I could finally track her down instead of waiting outside the shop like a fucking creeper.

"Be careful." She forced a sad smile. "I'm sure I'll see you very soon."

Something in her words caused a chill to run down my spine.

CHAPTER THREE

"Hey, you." The girl from earlier arched her eyebrow as I took my seat next to her.

Maybe I should've taken my chances with Connor. "Hi." Maybe she'd get the hint.

"I've decided I like you." She flipped her hair over her shoulder. "So, my name is Ella. You'll need to know my name for this to continue."

I grabbed my notebook and pencil out of my bag and leaned back in my seat, keeping my eyes forward.

"This is the part where you tell me your name." She turned her body toward me and tilted her head.

"Not interested." Maybe if I was blunt, she'd get the hint.

"Hmmm... I heard that guy holler it out in the last class, so technically I know it. But I'm going to pretend I don't until I hear it from you." She tapped her lips with her fingertip. "Then, I'll go with Hope. Because maybe if I call you that, you wouldn't have such a dark cloud over your head."

My lips twitched to inch upward, but I bit my tongue.

"Elena." Connor entered the room with a huge smile on his face. "You must not have seen me Monday. I saved you a seat." He pointed to the desk that was vacant beside where he had sat the other day.

"No, I saw you." He needed to get the damn hint. "Just didn't want to sit there."

"What?" His mouth dropped, and he shook his head. "Oh, you want to be in the back." He grinned at me once more. "I get that. I'll come join you."

He made his way to the open desk beside me. As he placed his black backpack down, his light blue polo shirt inched up, showing his six-pack.

I had to give him credit. He was hot in the wholesome, all-American way. He had short, dirty-blond hair and blue eyes.

As he slid into the seat, he grinned in my direction. "So... what are you doing later?"

"Gotta wash my hair." I'd rather go jump off a bridge than do anything with him.

"Oh, well, what about tomorrow?" He bit his bottom lip and scanned my body. "I'd like to pick up where we left off."

"Not interested." I wasn't sure how else to make it clear to him.

"That's the second time you've said that in two minutes." Ella giggled and shook her head. "I'm kind of offended you lumped me in with him."

"What the hell does that mean?" Connor frowned at her.

"She's not interested. Why don't you get a clue?" Ella rolled her eyes and shook her head. "You're panting after her like a puppy dog."

That was a fair analysis.

"Why don't you mind your own business?" Connor frowned at her.

Thankfully, the professor entered the room. His eyes settled on me for a second. "I'm so glad you made time for us again."

He was trying to embarrass me. "I'm punctual like that. I'm here when class begins and ends when the time on my schedule is up."

Ella snorted.

The professor startled and took a deep breath. "Well, I guess I better get to it."

As USUAL, I stood right at the class end time and began my trek out the door.

"Hey, Elena," Ella called after me.

"I thought I was Hope?" I couldn't keep the small grin off my face.

"Ha, well. Dumbass said your name, so I figured..." She stopped and pursed her lips. "I kinda like the nickname Hope. I mean, it pegs you hardcore."

"Did you catch up with me to insult me?" She had some balls, so I had to give her that. Most people tried to stay clear of me.

"Yeah, I figured you didn't hate yourself enough, so I thought I'd help you out."

We walked outdoors, and the breeze picked up. That's when her earthy scent hit me. Shit, she was a wolf shifter. No wonder I felt inclined to like her. "Well, don't worry. It's more than you probably can see." I had to get away and now.

"Look, I'm going to a party tonight." She shrugged her

shoulders and licked her lips. "I thought maybe you wouldn't mind keeping me company."

"That's a no." I already told her I wasn't interested, so I wasn't sure why she just asked the question. "If the 'I'm not interested' comment back there confused you, it meant no."

"See, there's something about you that intrigues me." She lifted both hands in the air. "I'm not into girls if that's what you're worried about."

A laugh escaped me before I could shut it down. "I'm so glad you clarified that."

"Just wanted to make sure I didn't give off those vibes." She waved her arm up and down my body. "Not that you aren't hot."

"Uh... thanks, I think." I stopped moving before I realized what I'd done. Dammit, she was going to be a problem. I didn't want friends.

"Where are you heading off to?" She glanced around. "You got another class?"

"In a couple of hours." I had history and composition later on. I'd been pissed when I couldn't get all my classes back to back, but there wasn't anything I could do about it.

"Let's go grab something to eat then." She took a few steps in the direction of the cafeteria.

"Uh... They probably aren't serving lunch."

"So?" She shrugged her shoulders and grabbed my arm, dragging me along with her. "We'll grab a coffee and wait. My next class starts at noon, so we can hang out for a little while."

For once, I didn't have a reason to say no. I didn't have a single damn thing to do, so I found myself following her.

It only took a few minutes before we entered the student center. It was only ten in the morning and was busy with students. There was a Starbucks inside, which surprised me.

"Let's go get that coffee before we sit down." She beelined straight to the coffee shop and got in line. "What are you going to get?"

"Uh... coffee?" It came out as a question when I hadn't meant for it to.

"You don't know." She patted my shoulder and winked. "I got you covered, girl."

"What can I get for you today?" The cashier glanced at both Ella and me.

"We'll take two grande blonde lattes with nonfat milk and vanilla." She rambled the words off her lips as if she was a pro.

"Got it." The lady typed in the order on the cash register. "Name?"

"Hope." She grinned as she glanced at me from the corner of her eyes.

She sure was something. I had to admit I might've deserved that.

"All right." The girl smiled. "It'll be ready in a minute."

"Come on, grumpy." Ella waved me over to the pick-up side. "Let's hope this turns some of the grumpiness into at least mildly cordial."

It was damn refreshing to be around someone who said what they thought. But I didn't need to get close for two reasons. One; caring made you vulnerable; and two; she was a shifter. The witch had warned that being around others like me would cause my wolf side to give me more problems.

"You're going to love this drink." She grinned and rubbed her hands together. "It's my weakness."

"I'm not even sure I know what to expect." I shook my head and sighed. "When did drinks become blonde?"

"They're a lighter brew with a caramel taste." She bumped her shoulder into mine. "Damn, you're freaking stout."

"That could be considered an insult." The last thing I needed her to do was make a big deal about how strong I was. Any shifter should've been able to at least nudge a human. "I work out a lot." That wasn't a lie either, so technically, I didn't have to feel bad.

"Obviously." She scanned my arms and legs. "I bet you could take my brother."

"Ha." Now I regretted coming. I should've known better.

"No, seriously." Her eyes lit up as our drinks were placed on the counter. "He's kind of the rebel. You know Mason?"

"No, I don't know Mason." I had way too little time to deal with rebels or anyone for that matter. "But good for you."

"Seriously?" She took a step closer to me, and a smirk crossed her face. "He's the guy on campus that everyone wants."

"Uh... congrats." I had no clue what to say in awkward situations like these. Wait... I'd never been in a situation like this.

She laughed so loud it hurt my ears. "Why are you congratulating me?"

"You seem awfully proud that everyone wants your brother and that he's a rebel." I grabbed my latte and took a sip. It was fucking delicious.

Ella smiled so wide that I could probably see every one of her teeth. "You like it." She took a large sip and closed her eyes. "That proves we're going to be besties."

"What?" I choked on the sip I just took.

"Boy, do you have commitment issues." She rolled her eyes. "I wasn't asking for your hand in marriage."

"I don't do friends." I made a mistake coming here.

"Good thing I'm not asking you to do me." She reached out and patted my shoulder.

"That's not what I meant." I struggled not to let the smile grow across my face. It'd been a very long time since this had been an issue.

"Doesn't matter." She looped her arm through mine and tugged me toward the tables. "You're stuck with me."

"Hey, Ella," a guy called as we passed by. He ran his fingers through his chestnut-brown hair and pulled out a seat at the table. "Why don't you two join me here?"

"We were going to have girl talk." She tugged me on, but he stepped in front of us and pouted.

"Are you coming to the bar tonight?" His green eyes stayed locked on her. "The whole... group is going." His tight shirt emphasized his muscular build, and he had to be close to six feet tall.

"You know I hate going. They refuse to serve me alcohol." She sighed and rolled her eyes.

"Bring your friend here." His gaze landed on me. "She looks to be a freshman. There. Problem solved."

"Hell, yeah." She turned to face me and grinned. "I mean you do owe me one after the coffee."

"No... I'd better not." I had a date with Netflix tonight, so they were shit out of luck.

"Aw, come on." He reached over and touched my arm. "It's a group of our friends, and we behave for the most part."

I jerked back. I didn't like being touched. "Doesn't really sound like my scene."

"What?" He laughed as his forehead furrowed. "It's every college student's scene."

"Maybe when they're drinking age." She rolled her eyes and sighed. "Mason makes sure they know I'm underage. The one thing I wish he'd be chill over, and he's not."

"Having a brother who cares must suck." Her strange comments amused me. "Though it sounds fun, I have homework I need to get done."

"Please." She pouted and gave me her puppy dog eyes. "I'll pick you up and everything. Hell, I'll buy your dinner."

"I'm sorry but no." I couldn't abandon my whole life's motto of keeping my distance from everyone, especially supernaturals, now. "I'm sure you can find someone else to go with you."

"Ugh, but they are so boring and only after my brother." She whined and pouted.

"Sorry, good luck with all that." This was my cue to leave. "Hey, I forgot I had to run an errand before my class later. I'll see you around." I spun on my heel, taking off before she could convince me to stay.

"Elena," she yelled after me, but all I did was stick my hand up to wave goodbye.

When I stepped outside of the student center, my breathing finally returned to normal. I hadn't realized how claustrophobic I felt until I took a deep breath of clean air.

There was a group of people standing in front of the student center, laughing as I walked by. They smelled human with no supernatural in the mix.

It sucked because I'd give anything to be just like them. Human, normal, no knowledge of the supernatural, and only caught up in who's doing what. They didn't realize how lucky they were to be born that way.

I headed toward my history class. It started in thirty

minutes, but I figured maybe there wasn't anyone around and I could go ahead and get my seat.

As I moved in that direction, I felt a buzzing in my pocket. I pulled my phone out and saw a text from the bar I worked at.

Can you come and fill in for Suzy tonight?

That was the third time Brad had asked me to cover for her in the last two weeks. It paid the bills though and gave me something else to do. So I replied yes and shoved it back into my pocket.

It didn't take long for me to reach the building, and as I stepped into the hallway, a guy with short dark hair and piercing green eyes walked past me.

My world seemed to stand still for that moment, but he didn't glance my way. He rushed out of the building on some kind of mission or something.

I took a few steps, following him, when I realized what the hell I was doing. I'd lost my damn mind. I stopped and watched him run off toward the student center.

It probably was a good thing that I hadn't stayed there. If Ella had seen my reaction, I was sure she would've wound up doing something to embarrass me.

Making myself turn around, I began my slow stroll through the hallway, looking for the class. After a few minutes, I found it on the fourth floor of the building.

It was empty, so I headed straight to the back, taking the center-aisle to the desk right in the corner. It was the easiest spot to hide. The only problem was when teachers would go overtime and I left. There was something about punctuality that had been ingrained in me. You arrive on time and leave on time. At least that's how I'd been raised.

I pulled out my phone as it vibrated again. It was Brad again.

Good, there is a huge business party coming in, so be ready to haul ass.

Great. That meant tonight was going to suck. Usually, large parties included some kind of supernatural. It made it rough to pretend to be human because there was a scent all supernaturals had. Granted, I never shifted, so it shouldn't be a problem, but you never know who you might run into.

CHAPTER FOUR

I put on my standard black shirt and blue jeans that were dress code for the bar. In all fairness, it was a trendy bar that businesses and more upper-class individuals liked to frequent.

It was a large open space with a huge bar in the center. The bar faced the open area, and there was a glass wall right behind it.

There were tables set up outside with a cover, and inside were more tables spread throughout. In the middle of the seating, there was a winding staircase that connected to the top floor. Up on the top floor was where all the pool tables, dartboards, and lounge seating were held.

"We better get some good tip money tonight," Todd grumbled as he put on the apron over his dark shirt. He was only a few years older than me, but he complained about everything, and that was saying something, coming from me.

"As long as you put a smile on your face and keep the negativity to yourself, you should be good." To say he hated when I called him out would be an understatement.

"It wouldn't kill you to be nice every now and then." He arched an eyebrow and tied the strings in the back.

"It might." Being nice to people encourages them to hang around you more. That's what I was trying to avoid.

"In all fairness, if you started being nice, it would freak me the fuck out." Todd rolled his dark chocolate eyes at me. "I've grown oddly attached to your pessimistic vibe."

"Not pessimistic." I grabbed a clean towel and began wiping down the beer glasses. "Realistic."

"That's what all pessimistic people say." He grabbed his notebook and pen. "Shouldn't you be the one serving all those bureaucratic men?" He nodded toward the door where a group of at least twenty-five men dressed in suits stood.

"I don't do people well." Now, that wasn't an exaggeration. I purposely went out of my way to not talk to people. That's the reason I chose to work in the kitchen instead of a club. I made a little less, but I didn't have sloppy, drunk-ass men hitting on me.

"You better be glad Brad cares that you're underage, or he'd have your hot ass serving drinks." He took a deep breath as if he was gearing up for the jackasses.

All men in suits were jackasses. I learned that at the tender age of six. And in all fairness, he couldn't allow me to waitress. He'd tried, but I refused to get certified to serve drinks. "Don't let them be complete dicks."

He winked at me and nodded toward the large table that the hostess was pushing together. "Wish me luck."

Considering the way that group looked, he was going to need more than luck. I left the bar area and moved back toward the kitchen. The last thing I wanted to do was get stuck serving them drinks. "Why don't you go back there and start washing dishes?" Brad walked out from his back office and looked at me. "They never got caught up after the lunch rush, and I'm thinking we're going to have another round to do after the dinner rush."

"Sure." Though it was disgusting, that was one of the jobs I preferred. I didn't have to talk to coworkers to accomplish it. I moved over to the four large industrial dishwashers and began scraping the plates and loading them up.

"ELENA," Todd called my name, startling me from my task. "Can you help me serve their food?"

"Oh, yeah." I wanted to say no, but I was pretty sure that wouldn't go over well. I washed my hands and turned to help him carry the food out.

I grabbed four plates and followed behind Todd. As we began passing out food, an overly sweet smell hit my nose.

That could only mean one thing. At least one out of this group was a vampire.

Even if I hadn't been able to narrow it down to the guy on the end, the fact that he was the only one that didn't order any food would have put a nail in the coffin. I tried putting on a sincere smile as I turned to him. "Oh, what did you order? I'll go check on it for you."

The man turned his cold blue eyes on me and smirked. "I do intermittent fasting and can't eat past four." He looked to be in his mid-thirties and was on the thin side like most vampires were. He tugged at the knot on his tie and nodded. "But thank you for checking." His eyes scanned me from head to toe.

"No problem." I hated being close to vampires. The whole point of the wolves was to keep all supernaturals in line, especially the vampires. They were the one race who the wolves warred with most often since they all tended to be self-absorbed and heartless. Mom had believed that it was because their hearts didn't beat.

I forced myself to pass him. I'd always been taught to never turn your back on one of them. They were often unpredictable and could change their moods as quickly as the wind changed directions.

Footsteps followed behind me.

If I didn't have wolf ears, I wouldn't have been able to hear him. Not able to stop myself, I turned in his direction. "Oh." I tried to act surprised, but it fell short.

"Why am I not surprised you heard me?" He narrowed his eyes and tapped his pointer finger on his lips. "I just can't figure out quite what you are."

"I'm a waitress here." In order to act human, it was integral to pretend that you knew nothing of the supernatural world. "And I felt a cold chill down my spine. That's why I turned around. How did you walk that quietly?"

His face was a mask of indifference. "Your movements are too agile to be human." He smirked and tilted his head. "There's something odd that I can't place. You don't have any specific characteristics that tell me what you are. But there is a hint of something that I can't quite capture."

"As riveting as this is, I've got to go back to work." I needed space from this jackass and fast. "If you think of anything you need, I'm only a few feet away." I forced myself to turn around again and slowly head back to the kitchen. I couldn't let him know how bad he bothered me.

The last thing I needed was to intrigue a vampire and have them dig into my existence any further.

WHEN THE CLOCK HIT TEN, I clocked out and headed toward my car. The restaurant was open for another hour, but the kitchen help normally was able to get out a little earlier as long as the dishes were caught up.

The restaurant would've been dead if we didn't have the business party here. I tended to like the nights when things moved at a slower pace. This place was too expensive for most of the college kids. My heart hammered as I hurried to my vehicle. The vampire probably had forgotten all about me, but you could never be careless.

As soon as I made it into my car and locked the doors, my heart began to steady. Thank God I'd been overreacting.

Within fifteen minutes, I pulled into my driveway. I grabbed my purse and locked the car door, marching straight into the house.

"How was your day?" Mona laid on the couch, sprawled out.

"Good. Long." I sighed and removed my shoes at the door. "How about you two?"

Kassie was in her usual spot on the recliner. She paused the television and glanced my way. "Mine was fine. The later breakfast crowds are always fun, so I'm tired as usual."

She'd been complaining about the college kids rushing in near lunchtime, wanting a combination of breakfast and lunch options, for the past eight years.

"The shop had some good visitors today." Mona yawned and stretched out her arms. "I had a few witches come in, looking for some things."

"That's never a good sign." Kassie shook her head. "At least we're not all involved in that shit anymore."

"You never know." Mona darted her eyes in my direction. "Before long, we may be in all that again."

"How many times do I have to tell you that I don't want

the crown?" Besides, they'd raised me to take care of myself now. I could take down a wolf twice my size. That wasn't very royal-like.

"We know." Mona shrugged and pointed to the kitchen. "I put some steak up from dinner. Do you want me to warm it for you?"

"Nope, I've got it." I made my way into the kitchen and opened the refrigerator door.

It didn't take long for me to eat, and I headed to bed.

───

BEFORE I KNEW IT, Friday had come back around. I hurried into the classroom and sat in my usual seat.

I got here a little earlier than normal, beating most of the class. I'd had trouble sleeping again last night, but that wasn't so strange lately. I decided to get up and head on in.

"Hey, I'm glad to see you here early." Connor dropped his bag at his normal seat but came over and sat next to me. "I'd permanently move but one of my close buddies is in here with me. He gave me shit the other day for changing seats."

"No, it's fine." That was the last thing I wanted him to do. "I just wanted to get here and get some early reading done today." I pulled my textbook out of my bag and hoped he'd get the hint.

"You got all weekend for that." He rolled his eyes and leaned uncomfortably close to my chair. "So you got any weekend plans?"

"Yeah, it's going to be busy." That wasn't close to being true, but that was my story, and I was sticking to it.

"Oh, are you going to any parties or anything?" He cleared his throat and tugged at his ear.

"That's not really my thing." The one time I'd let loose, I slept with him, and look where that got me. The girl that was showing me around campus made sure the party was our last stop, and I figured what the hell. Which only proved how much I wasn't made for friends. I didn't need any clingers. Supernatural or not.

"But that's where we met." He laughed like I'd told some sort of joke.

"Well, that was my first and last time."

"But I could take you to this one." He smirked and winked at me.

All right, blunt it would be. "You're kind of the reason I don't go anymore."

"What?" His mouth dropped open, and he tilted his head.

At this point, he reminded me of a dog. "Yeah, I don't normally do that." I had to cut the cord.

"Hey, no. It's fine." His eyes lit up like a kid's on Christmas morning. "I can take you as my date. You don't have to worry about a one-night stand or anything."

Dear God. He was a fucking moron. "No, you're not getting what I'm trying to say."

"She doesn't do clingers." Ella entered the room with a huge smile on her face.

"I'm not clinging." He huffed and raised both hands up.

"What do you call this?" She pointed to the book I had open on my desk. "She's got her textbook out, trying to read instead of talking to you."

He wasn't understanding the clues from me. I'd only given him my phone number so I could escape and never responded to any of his texts. To top it all off, I ignored him when I saw him in this class and avoided him to the best of my abilities. Maybe she could get through to him.

"She's just playing hard to get." His face kind of fell, and he glanced at me. "Right?"

"No, sorry." I couldn't lie and try to tell him it was me and not him. "We're just not right for each other."

"But we just had sex..." He jerked back as if he'd been burned. "Are you saying I wasn't a good lay?"

"I'm really trying not to." But he was about to force my hand. I was trying not to embarrass the guy.

"So, since you're having trouble breaking it down." Ella plopped in her seat beside me. "That means yes. You weren't good."

"I was drunk." He spoke louder despite the fact students were beginning to trickle in. "Let's do a sober do-over. You'll see."

"No, I won't." He reminded me of the type of guy who always got what he wanted and never had to work at anything. He probably never had to handle rejection like this before.

"In other words, not interested." Ella shook her head and gazed at me. "Be glad I'm here to be your wingwoman."

"That's usually for picking up guys." She beat to her own drum, and I liked it.

"Eh, it's for everything. Pick-ups and dumps." She lifted a finger in the air. "Not to be confused with bowel movements."

"Noted." Even though I couldn't stand Connor, I didn't want to steamroll him, and class should be starting any second. I took a deep breath and leaned toward him, lowering my voice, "You weren't bad."

"I wasn't?" There was hope glowing in his eyes. "Then, what's the problem?"

"There wasn't a connection." He had been boring as hell, but I was sure, for a true human, he'd been excellent.

I'd had a few sexual encounters, and most of them had been the same way. I was betting it was because whether I liked it or not, I was a wolf. "That's it."

"But I..." He trailed off and took a deep breath. "Okay, got it."

"It looks like you kicked his puppy or something," Ella whispered, probably not realizing I could hear it.

"Thanks for the talk?" Though he had meant it as a statement, the tone ended on a question as if he wasn't sure.

"Yeah, I'm glad we're on the same page finally." I needed him to leave me alone now.

"You have a break between classes, right?" Ella pulled out her notebook and pen.

"Uh, yeah." She couldn't be trying to talk me into going to the student center with her again.

"How long of a break do you have?" She tapped her pen on her paper.

"About an hour." I didn't want to hang out on campus, but at the same time, I didn't have time to leave campus either.

"There's a coffee shop a few blocks away." She leaned toward me and winked. "It's right by the university; not in it. Why don't we go hang out over there?"

"I'm not sure..."

"Where are you going to go? Sit in the other classroom for an entire hour?" She tilted her head toward me and arched an eyebrow. "We both know that it'd be more fun if you spent time with me."

That was precisely the problem. I didn't mind her company. "Fine, but as long as it's not on campus."

I agreed, but I couldn't help but wonder if I was making a big mistake.

CHAPTER FIVE

The next few weeks seemed to pass in a blur. Even though I tried fighting Ella's friendship, she'd completely lured me in. She was funny, blunt, and a breath of fresh air.

We stood from our desks as we both walked out into the hallway together. "Coffee shop again, or are we ready to brave the Student Center once more?"

"Coffee shop." She'd been mentioning the student center more and more lately.

"Ugh, fine." She pouted. "It's just that the coffee shop is so much farther to my next class."

"So, you're getting lazy on me?" She had yet to tell me about being supernatural, which I didn't blame her for. Hell, I hadn't told her about me being one either.

"Hey, it's hard to be so put together." She flipped her hair over her shoulder as she snorted. "I can't keep rushing to class. I get all sweaty."

"I'm sure you can handle it." I had a feeling eventually she was going to wear me down.

"Ella." A deep, raspy voice echoed in the hallway.

"Great." She huffed and turned to face the person head-on.

I took a few steps off toward the side and continued my march to the front of the building. That was until Ella grabbed my arm.

"Don't you dare try to sneak off. This won't take long."

"Hey." The guy I'd seen in the hallway that day after I ran from the student center was standing right in front of me. His eyes darted to me and kept hold. "Who are you?"

"Nobody." A shiver wanted to rock through my body.

"You sure don't look like a nobody." A small grin peeked through the corner of his lips.

"No! Do not hit on her." Ella stepped in between us and pointed her finger at him. "She is my friend, and you better back off."

"What?" He stepped around to look at me once more. "I mean, I should know your friends, right?"

The bastard was hot and arrogant. I should be disgusted, but my damn body was responding to him in very inappropriate ways. I had no clue who he was, but he was definitely a shifter, which meant that was not good. "Nah, I think you'll be fine letting me keep my secrets."

"Maybe I..."

"Mason, stop." All humor was removed from her face. "Seriously, she's my friend. One I don't want to share with you because then when you break her heart, she'll not want to be my friend anymore."

Something passed through his eyes. "Hey, that's not true..." He winced and nodded his head. "Fine, since you asked so lovingly."

I couldn't believe this was her brother, and of course, he'd be a womanizer. "Glad we're all three settled on that." I turned my back to him and nodded at Ella. "I'll wait for you out front."

"Yeah, okay." Her shoulders seemed to sag a little. "Be there in a second."

After I was a few steps away, Mason whispered to Ella. "Who the hell is she?"

Of course, they hadn't realized I was a shifter and that I could hear them from this distance.

"Seriously, she's one of my friends." Her tone took on an edge. "So don't mess with her. For once, someone wants to be my friend for me."

"All right." He huffed.

"Stop looking at her." I heard a loud thump.

"Dammit. Okay."

If I had any doubt they were related, that would've been erased now. I headed outside, effectively cutting their conversation off from my ears.

It was a gorgeous day, and I moved over to a vacant bench and sat.

"Hey, Elena." Connor waved and headed over in my direction.

Great, maybe I should've stayed inside and eavesdropped on Ella and her brother. "Hi."

"How is class going for you?" He glanced at the ground and adjusted his backpack straps on his shoulders.

"Fine." It was a straightforward business ethics class. "How about you?" The tension between us was thick.

"Boring, but okay." He cleared his throat and darted his eyes to mine. "Would you wanna have coffee or something sometime?"

"We've already had this conversation." At this point, I wasn't sure how much more blunt I could be. "I'm not interested."

"I mean as friends." He scratched the back of his neck with his hand.

"Still no." I guessed I was going to have to be a bitch. "I don't think you mean that."

"No, I do." He lifted both hands in the air and tensed his shoulders. "You made it blatantly clear, but I'd like to have you in my life in some capacity."

"Are you really trying to work the friend angle?" Ella breezed through the doorway and sat right next to me. "I thought you'd at least be a little more original than that."

"He says he's okay with being friends." I arched an eyebrow at her. "Do you believe it?"

"Hell, no." She motioned toward my body. "You're hot stuff, so he's trying to find another way in."

"What? No." He shook his head until Ella crossed her arms.

"If you want to be her friend, that means you want to be mine too." She bumped her shoulder into mine. "It's a package deal."

"Uh, sure." He tilted his head and squinted his eyes for a moment. "Of course I want to be friends with both of you."

"So you're saying I have a hot body too?" She tilted her head and tapped her foot on the ground.

"What? No." Connor shook his head hard.

"Now I'm not hot?" She turned her head in my direction and widened her eyes. "He's not very nice, is he?"

"No, I didn't mean that."

Poor guy. Ella was having fun at his expense.

"Of course you didn't." She huffed and stood again. "Come on, let's go. We don't need to stay here all day and get insulted."

I would've felt bad for him if he hadn't brought it on

himself. But I didn't want to leave being an asshole. "Look, if you want to be friends that's fine. But I don't hang out or anything like that. Essentially, it's just you saying hi to me when I pass."

"Yeah, okay." His eyes focused back on the ground. "I just thought..."

"Thinking usually gets guys in trouble." Ella tugged on my arm ready to go. "So I'd recommend you stop right there."

"I'll see you later." I stood and followed Ella.

She stopped and waited for me to catch up. "He's trying to weasel his way in."

"Yeah, I know." That was pretty obvious. "It won't work, so don't worry."

"Oh, I wasn't." She shook her head and sighed. "It's just, how blunt do we have to be in order for him to realize it's not happening."

"As long as I'm single, he might think there's a chance." What he didn't realize was that I'd be single for my entire life.

"Then we need to find you a date." Her eyes sparkled. "Maybe he'll finally shut it down."

"I don't date." Never had and didn't ever plan on starting that.

"Heartbroken?" She frowned as she slowed her pace.

"Yeah, something like that." It wasn't from a guy tearing my heart out.

"That sucks." She looped her arm through mine. "Been there and done that."

"What happened?" The more I could get her talking about herself, the less it would be about me.

"Let's just say he found someone else." Her usual happy demeanor chilled.

"I'm sorry. He didn't deserve you." Whoever it was made an impact on her.

"It wasn't his fault. Sometimes, fate has a way of intervening." She sighed and stared off. "Some people were made for each other. I wasn't made for him."

He must have found his fated mate. "It still sucks, whether he meant it or not."

"Now that I can agree with."

The coffee shop appeared in front of us. We'd be there in a matter of minutes.

"Is your brother okay?" I hadn't meant to ask the question, but he kept appearing in my mind.

"Oh, yeah." She waved it off, but her feet slowed a little. "He made a decision that I'm not super thrilled with, and he wanted to let me know before I heard it from someone else."

"What is he doing?" If she wasn't thrilled, it couldn't be something good.

"He's doing something illegal." She opened the door to the coffee shop, and we both entered.

"It's not like," I said and then lowered my voice, "drugs or anything, right?"

She burst out laughing. "No. God no." She held her side and laughed some more. "Not like that. It's a little insane. He's doing some fighting in a gym. After-hours if you know what I mean."

"Okay." That wasn't too horrible, as long as he didn't get caught. The plus side was him being a shifter, so he shouldn't get hurt too badly.

"Don't get all judgmental on him." She pulled out her credit card as she approached the cash register. "Mom's not doing so well, and we need the money."

"I'm sorry." I wasn't sure what else to say. I wanted to ask if they notified the regional representatives, but then that would open up another can of worms. "Do you want me to like him or not?"

"What?" Her forehead furrowed.

"Your brother." She gave me hell all the time. "You threaten him to not talk to me and then get pissy when you think I'm criticizing him. Pick a side."

She stopped in her tracks and tapped her hands on her dress. "I'm not being pissy, it's complicated. Okay? I don't want something to happen and lose this."

"Fine." I still wasn't sure how to act with a friend without feeling weird. I sidled up to the register and ordered two vanilla lattes.

"Hey, I always get these." She swung her hip into mine, trying to get me to move away.

"Exactly. It's my treat." I had just gotten paid, and the tips were good from that huge party the other night, I wanted to at least buy this round. "Don't worry. I got paid."

"You work?" She tilted her head and examined me. "I don't know why, but I wasn't expecting that."

"Don't worry. I'm the kitchen help most of the time, so I get to be by myself, washing dishes, and don't have to interact with a lot of people." That was the top job require-ment when I started looking. Mona had wanted me to work in the antique store with her, but I didn't want to be around all those supernaturals. They tended to be her biggest customer base. Humans greatly underestimated the value of old relics.

"Good." She moved aside so I could hand the cashier my credit card. "You'd make a killing as a waitress if you could smile and be nice to people."

"Hey, I'm buying your drink right now."

"But I'm different." She pointed to her face and smiled. "My natural charm removes your natural defenses."

She was one hundred percent right, but I wouldn't admit it. "Eh... sure. Let's go with that."

"You bitch." She laughed though she tried to school her features into a mask of indifference.

"Please stop." I couldn't hold back my laughter. "You look constipated."

"Here you go." The cashier handed me back my card with a slight scowl on her face. "Next."

"I don't think she appreciated our swagger." Ella rolled her eyes with a huge grin on her face.

"Most don't." It felt so weird and nice to be like this with someone. In all reality, she was my first real friend.

Her phone buzzed, and she huffed. "Hey, I'm going to have to go and meet one of my brother's friends. There's something going on."

Our lattes got placed on the counter, and I walked over and grabbed both of them.

"Then go." I handed her coffee to her. "I'll see you next week."

"Are you working this weekend?" She took the drink from my hand and smiled. "And thank you for this."

"Yeah." I wasn't quite sure what she was aiming for.

"Dammit." She pouted and sighed. "I'll be tied up with my brother and his friends this weekend. All right, have a great weekend, and Monday we're back on schedule. Okay?"

"Got it." I watched her run out of the coffee shop and hoped that everything was okay.

As I hurried to my car, something cold ran down my spine. It felt as if I was being watched. As I walked past a section of trees right before my parking lot, a comforting earthy smell hit me, and all of a sudden Ella's brother stepped out.

His shirt wasn't tight, but the fit emphasized the muscles in his chest, and his gorgeous eyes landed on me. "What's the hurry? Are you being chased?" He grinned.

He probably thought he was being clever. Yeah, he was a wolf and thought I was unaware, but frankly, I was the one who had the upper hand. At least, for now... "Nope, just needing to get away from you." I turned on my heel, and as I walked past him, he reached out, snagging my arm.

"Most girls are flattered to receive my attention." He arched a perfectly sculpted eyebrow.

"Well, being stalked isn't flattering in my book." I yanked my arm away from him and tried not to shiver. His touch was way too pleasant, and it couldn't happen again. "So why don't you go spend your time on them and not me." I pushed my legs to walk fast, gaining distance between us, but he was watching me, so moving at a speed I wanted to wasn't a good idea.

"Hey," he yelled at me, but I ignored him as I hurried into the parking lot. Maybe he'd get the hint.

I ARRIVED at work only a few hours after my last class. I hurried into an already buzzing, packed building.

The one good thing about busy nights was there were a lot of dishes I had to scrape off and clean, so I should get out of having to do anything that involved peopling.

Not wasting any time, I clocked in and headed toward the kitchen.

"Thank God you're here." Brad pointed at the dish-washers. "All three of them just now stopped running. Fill them up and do the remainder by hand. We're in for a busier than normal night."

"Oh, what's going on?" We were always busy, but I normally didn't have a ton of dishes to wash by hand.

"We have the same business party and a rehearsal dinner." He walked into the back and put on an apron. "It's all hands on deck."

That was fine with me. I dug in and began working. It didn't take long for my arms to be elbow deep in soapy dishwater.

Thankfully, the night ended fast.

"Good job, everyone." Brad took off the apron and threw it in the dirty clothes hamper. "We somehow survived."

He hadn't been kidding when he said it was going to be crazy. I still had another two loads to fill.

"Let's go clean up the dining room while Elena finishes up here." The crew went into the dining room, leaving me and the other cook behind.

The cook was cleaning the kitchen while I focused on unloading and loading the dishwashers.

It didn't take terribly long to fill one of the machines when something dropped and rolled over to my feet.

My eyes dropped and landed on some kind of marble. I bent down to snag it off the ground. I picked it up and looked inside. It had a three-dimensional image of a triangle upside down with a line straight through the center. A circle partially arched into the center.

That was the ancient vampire symbol for danger.

I glanced around; looking for who dropped this, but there was no one in sight. The only evidence that it was, in fact, a vampire was the sweet, pungent air they'd left behind. It had to have been that guy from the party.

There was no other evidence that he was still around. Granted, my senses weren't as strong as a wolf that had shifted. I wasn't quite sure if someone was threatening me or warning me. Either way, it was disconcerting.

Feeling the need to get out of there, I moved fast, in a hurry to get home. Within the next five minutes, I was done and heading toward the door. "Hey, I'm done and need to be heading home."

Brad gave me a strange look but nodded. "Okay, we're done here. See you tomorrow."

I waved and ran out the door. I scanned the area again, but there wasn't anyone around. I forced myself not to run to the car because, if he was watching me, it would make me seem more like prey.

As I slammed the car door, something caught my eye in the woods. I examined the area, but other than the tree limbs swaying, there wasn't anything out of place. Needing distance, I pressed the gas, hauling ass home.

CHAPTER SIX

A chill ran through me as I threw on my jeans and a teal shirt. Even though I hadn't noticed a vampire since Friday, I couldn't shake the feeling of being watched. I had too much going on and probably needed to stay low-key.

Of course, it didn't help that it was Monday, so the week was only getting started. I yawned and put on enough makeup to hide my dark circles and ran the brush through my hair. I was off tonight, so I was hoping I'd get caught up on sleep. I glanced at the vampire marble that I'd placed in my jewelry box, attempting to hide it from my guardians.

It didn't take me long to grab something to eat and head out the door. I paused, scanning the area before climbing into my car and cranking the engine.

The past weekend had been a little intense. Between the vampire and how busy the bar had been, my mind hadn't been able to shut off.

Before I realized it, I was coasting into the school parking lot. I'd gotten here earlier than I had intended, but at least, the area was more crowded here.

I slowly grabbed my things and stood, enjoying the sun that warmed my face. There were only rare moments where I felt somewhat peaceful.

"Do you normally hang out here before class?" The familiar deep rasp of his voice caressed my mind.

"What?" I turned toward him and almost gasped for breath.

Sweat dripped down Mason's shirtless, muscular body, and my eyes skimmed over a large wolf paw print tattoo on his toned arm.

Drool had to be pooling at the corner of my mouth as I fought the urge to lick his body. I'd never been this attracted to someone before.

His emerald eyes scanned my face. "You got a problem?"

Ah, he was an alphahole. I could be one too. "You're the one who stopped, so what the fuck is your problem?"

"You need to learn your place." He straightened his shoulders and looked at me with cold regard.

The irony in that statement had me bursting out into laughter. He had no clue who he was talking to, which was a good thing. The fact that they couldn't sense my wolf was a blessing within the curse.

"Are you okay?" Concern flickered in Mason's eyes as he used his forearm to wipe the sweat from his brow.

"Yeah." I took a few deep breaths, trying to rein the crazy in. I couldn't blame him for looking so concerned. I straightened my shoulders and lifted my chin. "It's just hilarious to think that you would assume I was so easily intimidated."

He scowled and narrowed his eyes at me. "I don't have time for this shit."

"Good." I needed him gone and now. "You're looking kind of out of shape, so you may want to go for a little longer."

My eyes had to be playing tricks on me because I saw the corner of his mouth tilt up ever so slightly. "Is that so?"

"Yup, it's easy to see why you're running." I was lying like hell. If I was Pinocchio, I'd have a nose longer than the average-sized erect penis. He was damn fine and hot as hell.

"Well, then I better take off." He stayed there gazing at me, not moving an inch.

Neither one of us wanted to be there or leave. "All right. Have fun." I exhaled and forced my legs to move. I even prevented myself from turning around and glancing back at him.

Soon, I heard his footsteps getting farther and farther away.

Maybe if we could keep up our façade, it wouldn't be so bad not being with him. Hell, he may not even feel it, given the circumstances.

Flashes of Mason's shirtless body kept popping into my mind as I made my way to class. I'd never been this hot and bothered before, and I had to get my shit together. The last thing I wanted was Ella smelling the arousal in the air. I was sure I'd never live that down.

"Hey, are you feeling okay?" Connor seemed to appear out of thin air.

Great, that's how preoccupied I was with thoughts of Mason. If the vampire was following me, he could have easily stood right in front of me, and I wouldn't have noticed. "Yeah, sorry. I'm just super anxious about this test." I'd studied all day yesterday and had this test in the bag. Business ethics wasn't that difficult.

"I'm sure you've got this." He smiled ever so slightly and adjusted the straps of his backpack on his shoulders. "If you're that stressed, we could start a study group or something."

This guy didn't give up. I wasn't quite sure if I admired him or thought he was an idiot. "I work most evenings. Sorry."

"Oh, really?" He kicked at the ground. "Where at?"

Yeah, I didn't think this one through. "Oh, some restaurant-bar kind of place."

"Near campus?" He took a step closer to me.

"No, you should know how I am by now." I shrugged my shoulders. "Being around a ton of people isn't my thing, so a bar close to campus wouldn't be ideal."

"That's not true." He lifted his hand, and his forehead creased. "We met at a party here on campus."

"But that's not my usual." The saying 'first impressions last forever' rang in my ears. "I had just toured the campus, and the guide made your party the last stop. I hadn't planned on staying long." Even though I hadn't shifted, for some reason, I still had a feeling like a mild heat spell. Not as rough as a typical female shifter, but I got hot and bothered that night when I spotted Connor. He was damn fine, but now that my brain was fully functioning, I wasn't the least bit attracted to him.

"You seemed to have a good time that night." His eyes lingered on my lips.

"Do we need to have that conversation over again?" Obviously, I couldn't be the least bit nice to him. "I'm not interested in you. I don't want you to come by my work."

"I feel like this is déjà vu." Ella's floral scent hit me as she walked up beside me. "She isn't into you."

"We were talking about our test." Connor cleared his

throat and glanced toward the building. "I guess we better get in so we aren't late."

"Right behind you," Ella called out as she grabbed my arm. "You must be amazing in bed."

"What?" I hadn't expected those to be the next words out of her mouth. "Why?"

"That boy is hard up for another round in the hay with you." She laughed and shook her head. "You must be magical in the sack."

"Hay? Sack? What are you? I don't think people our age talk like that anymore." That sounded like something Mona or Kassie would say. "Next time, you're going to say ride 'em cowgirl or bumpin' uglies."

"First off, please don't ride him." Ella looped her arm through mine and began our stroll to the building. "The one ride you gave him has him jonesing for more."

"Really?" She must be watching an older sitcom or something.

"Yes, really." She winked at me as she snorted. "But I kinda do like bumping uglies."

"Why am I not surprised?" It was nice to have someone to just go back and forth with.

"Sex is extremely satisfying if done right." A slow grin spread across her face. "Am I right?"

"Wouldn't know."

"Oh, we'll have to fix that." She placed her free hand on her chest. "That will be a top priority."

"No, our top priority is doing well on this exam." I quickened our pace. "So let's go do that, okay?"

"Fine, but afterward, we are going to need to talk about this." She shook her head and glanced at the ground. "This is something that we need to remedy as soon as possible."

The last thing I needed was her focusing on my sex life. It wasn't like I didn't have enough on my plate.

———

I MADE sure Ella finished her test before me. That way, I wouldn't hear the end of not waiting for her. She always needed to be on the go, so I should be home free for the next two days.

Not wasting any time, I turned in the test to the professor and walked out the door.

"I'm a little scared." Ella's voice echoed in the hall.

No, she wasn't supposed to be here. "What are you doing?"

"Waiting for you." She lifted both hands, and then she lifted her head with a huge smile on her face. "You didn't think I'd wait."

"Shh." I glanced back in the room, and the professor frowned at me.

"Come on," I whispered the words as I grabbed her arm, tugging her into the hallway. "You were being too loud."

"Aw, he'll get over it." She took a deep breath and stopped for a second. "Are you wearing a new perfume?"

"No, why?" That was an odd question.

"There's a hint of a sweet scent on you." Her eyes went straight to my neck. "Just curious."

That was not comforting. She must've suspected it was a vampire. "No. Maybe Kassie or Mona bought a different detergent." I may need to have a conversation with them and inform them about the weird-ass vampire.

"Yeah, maybe." She frowned and glanced at my neck again. "Do you mind if we go to the student center today?"

"What? No." I figured it was going to be brought up again soon.

"Please, I need to grab my textbook for the next class." She pouted and batted her eyes. "We never have to go again."

"Fine." One more time couldn't hurt me. "But in and out."

"Well, coffee first, and then we grab the textbook." She glanced at her phone. "We got out a little early, so we have time."

"Then the latte is on you today." I should've gotten some kind of compensation for emotional damage.

"Ugh, fine." She grinned as she rolled her eyes. "Drama queen."

"So you've dropped Hope completely now, and you're just going with Queen." I cringed as soon as the last word fell from my mouth.

"Nah, you'll always be Hope in my heart." She led me in the direction of the student center.

It didn't take us long to grab our lattes, and soon we were searching for her friend.

"It took you long enough." A guy called out from a corner table. He ran his fingers through his chestnut hair and grinned.

"Oh, bite me." Ella marched over to him and held out her hand for the book.

As soon as I got close to him, his pine scent hit my nose. He was definitely a wolf shifter too.

"Did I just get permission?" He waggled his eyebrows at her.

"Stop, you'll scare Elena away." She turned toward me and pointed to the guy. "Elena, this is Alec."

"You're the new friend she keeps talking about." His

charcoal eyes locked on mine. "It's kind of nice to match the face with a name. Even Mason has grumbled about you a time or two."

I wished he hadn't told me that. "Hi."

"Have you hit her up about tonight?" He glanced at Ella.

"No, I figured she would say no." She shook her head, making her blonde hair bounce. "But do you want to? Mason has another fight tonight."

"What? No." I had to keep my distance despite the fact that my wolf was clawing to see him again.

"Please come." Alec reached over and touched my arm. "I'm begging you. She chatters nonstop, and I could use a break."

"Hey." She reached over and smacked him. "It's actually pretty cool to watch."

"What kind of fighting is it? Boxing?" When she said gym, that was the first thing that had popped into my mind.

"Hell, no." The guy grabbed his backpack from the table and placed an arm through it. "MMA all the way."

"No way." Part of my training growing up was watching fights to see how to handle hand to hand combat.

"Yeah." He nodded his head. "If you get near the front, blood can splatter all down your shirt."

"Ew." Ella wrinkled her nose and smacked him in the arm. "You're doing an awful job recruiting her."

In all actuality, he was making it harder for me to say no. I enjoyed watching fights.

"Okay, then how about this..." He lifted his hand and lowered his head slightly to my side. "Muscular, shirtless guys."

"But they're wearing pants." Ella touched my arm and

leaned in. "Otherwise, I wouldn't be comfortable watching my brother fight naked."

"He said shirtless, not naked." Sometimes I wondered about her mind.

"Look, I can come pick you up, and we can grab some food beforehand." She grinned at me and clenched her hands into fists in excitement.

"This is beginning to sound more like a date than a fight."

"If you guys go home together, can I come and watch?" Alec wiggled his eyebrows at us suggestively.

"That's a no." Ella snorted and bumped into me. "Please, will you go?"

"Yes." The word fell out of my mouth before I could control it.

"Yay! We'll be there." Ella sat in the seat Alec just vacated. "There is no backing out now."

Great, just what I wanted.

———

"Where are you heading out to?" Mona stepped from the kitchen into the den.

"Oh, I have some errands to run." I never left the house unless it was for food, the witch, or supplies. However, none of them would take as long as I'd be, and I hated lying to them anyway.

"Let's see, your hair has recently been brushed. You have on a royal blue blouse and dark jeans." Her attention turned to my feet. "And you're wearing something other than tennis shoes. What's up?"

"Fine." I couldn't lie to them, but I could definitely omit

some parts. "I'm going out to dinner with a girl from school and maybe do something after."

"Hot damn. Has the girl actually made a sane decision?" Kassie walked into the room with a beer in hand. She moseyed over to the worn, leather couch and sat. "I'm kind of proud of you."

"Honestly, I got suckered into it somehow." The worst part was that I hadn't been completely dreading it.

"Good." Mona sat next to Kassie and grabbed the remote. "I hope she suckers you into more. You need friends and to have a life."

"Why do I need anyone else when I have you two?" They were the only ones I was letting into my life this close, and really, I didn't have much control over a decision with them. They'd taken care of me and had become the parents I needed. I would've been in foster care without them.

"That's very sweet but very worrisome." Mona pointed at me. "We're in our mid-forties. You just became an adult. You need friends that are closer to your age."

"So, is this how you're breaking up with me?" I loved ragging them.

"Hell, no." Kassie waved me off. "We're saying you need to add to your circle, not take away from it."

"Well, see, I'm going out tonight.' I glanced at my phone. She should be here in ten minutes. "I better go outside and wait for her." They knew I was strange when it came to boundaries, and right now I didn't want her to come in. That seemed too much for me at the moment.

"Fine, stay out late and have fun," Kassie hollered as I shut the door.

Those ladies were crazy sometimes.

I paused and took a deep breath. My nerves were running everywhere. Being nervous made me anxious.

Forcing my legs to move, I stumbled outside to wait for Ella to show up, which should have been any second. It wasn't long before a dark red Corolla pulled up right in front of me.

Ella rolled the window down and grinned. "Come on. Let's go eat. I'm starving."

"Yeah, okay." I climbed into her car and hoped I wouldn't regret this before the night was over.

CHAPTER SEVEN

W hen we pulled into a parking spot at the Mexican restaurant, my breathing quickened. This had to be a bad idea. Anything that made me this anxious couldn't be a good thing.

"Are you okay?"

My body startled as though I'd forgotten I was in her car. My eyes jerked over, and adrenaline pumped through my blood.

Her forehead lined with worry, and she tilted her head. "I just scared the shit out of you. Do you need to go home and change?"

I hated that I was that transparent. "Be glad that I don't. It could have easily gone the other way."

"You are so refreshing." She snorted. "So much better than all the other losers that tend to hang around us." She motioned for me to come with her. "Let's eat so we don't miss the fight."

"Yeah, all right." I rolled the window up and took a deep breath. I had to force myself to climb out.

"I have a feeling you'll like it here." She ran her fingers

through her hair as if it was out of sorts. It contrasted against her midriff black shirt and tight blue jeans.

She opened the door and waved me through. "Since you're my date, I better treat you nice."

"If you want me to put out, you'd better behave." She brought out a playfulness I thought I'd never find.

"Ha. You can't resist me." She sashayed up to the hostess. "Table for two."

"Okay." The woman bent down to grab some menus and gestured for us to follow her.

Honestly, I hadn't been out to a restaurant since God knows when. It was packed, and most of the people appeared to be college students like us.

As I passed a table of guys, one of them stood up and stepped in my way. "Hey, gorgeous." His eyes seemed to be undressing me right here in the middle of the restaurant.

I ignored him and moved to walk around him.

"Hey." He grabbed my arm, yanking me toward him. "I was talking to you."

"And I don't want to talk to you, so why don't you back off." This was why I stayed home. I didn't have to deal with idiots.

His buddies laughed.

"That's kind of cold." The stench of beer almost gagged me.

"Hey, baby." Connor's voice echoed in my ear. "Sorry I'm late."

I turned around to see him heading in the direction we'd just come from, sauntering straight to me. "Uh... hey."

He placed his hand on the guy's chest and pushed him into the seat. "Better luck next time. This one is mine." He took my hand in his and tugged me in the direction Ella had been heading.

The desire to jerk my hand out of his overwhelmed me. I didn't like being touched by anyone. As soon as we were out of their sights, I removed my hand. "What the hell was that?" My voice was a loud whisper.

"Usually, this is where you'd thank me." Connor smirked and shook his head. "But you're not like other girls."

"Look, I hate to do this to you and all, but she's my date tonight." Ella appeared beside me and arched an eyebrow. "So back the fuck off."

"Whoa." he lifted both hands in the air. "I'm not trying to interfere. You two go have your girl talk. I was just trying to help. The girl I'm with is waiting in the lobby."

"Are you serious?" I couldn't believe what he just said.

"What? Am I supposed to wait and pine for you or something?" The corners of his mouth twitched upward.

"Is that what you think this is about?" First off, I could've handled that asshole though Connor probably helped prevent me from making a scene, but still... "I can't believe you left her and acted like you were with me. Did she see you do that?"

"No, I told her I had to go to the bathroom." Any signs of a grin vanished.

"You are an ass." Ella laughed. "Go make up with the girl you brought and stop drooling over the one you want. It makes some of us uncomfortable." She glanced at the ceiling and tilted her head. "Actually, no. It brings me amusement in my life."

"Uh... Connor?" A girl with long black hair walked toward us. She wore a tank top with a low neckline, and she crossed her arms right under her breasts. "What's going on here?"

Thank God. This was going to be our saving grace. "He

was just telling us he needed to get back to you." I forced a smile that I hoped wasn't as awkward as it felt. "He saved me from some drunken asshole."

"Oh." Her shoulders relaxed, and she dropped her hands by her sides. "That was nice of him. Are you guys friends or something?"

"Uh..." His mouth dropped open, and his eyes glanced everywhere.

"Kinda." The idiot thought I was going to tell her we slept together. That had to be what it was. Otherwise, he was acting more awkward than I was, and that was saying something.

"We all three have a class together." Ella stepped forward and held her hand out. "I'm Ella, and this here is Elena." She turned back to Connor. "Thanks so much. We don't want to keep you away from your date any longer." She grabbed my arm and nodded toward a table for two. "We're here."

Not saying anything else to him, I turned and took my place at the table. There were already chips and salsa waiting for us. "I'm starving."

"Girl, me too." She sat on the other side and chuckled. "He's got it bad for you."

"Worst mistake of my life." I grabbed a tortilla chip and dipped it in the chunky salsa. "And we had absolutely no chemistry, so it makes it that much worse."

"He obviously disagrees." She rolled her eyes and took a sip of water. "If you'd asked him to sit with us, he would've dropped her like a bad habit."

"Well, good thing I didn't offer then." If I could've gone back in time to change the decision I made the night of the party, I would have. It wasn't long until we ordered and the waitress brought our food.

THE ENTIRE WAY to the fight, I was torn between anxiety and intrigue. I'd always enjoyed a good fight, but I had never seen one unless it had been on television. Before I knew it, we'd arrived.

It was a standalone building off a back road. The parking lot was huge in the back and couldn't be seen from the road. Almost every spot was taken, but Ella made herself a spot near the front, blocking in two cars.

"Don't you think you should move?" Someone might try to leave before we got out of there.

"God no. We'll probably leave before everyone else does." She shrugged and locked her door. "Come on, let's go get a seat."

I couldn't believe that the parking lot was so full. We headed toward the back, and I turned around to glance at everything one more time. "It's dark back here."

"Because they don't want the cops to see." She pushed the door open and walked in with little regard to all the bodies that were in our way. "Once we get closer to the ring, you'll be able to see better."

Apparently, I'd thrown my whole life plan to stay off the radar into the wind tonight. "It looks like there is a line."

"Girl, no." She took my hand and kept weaving through the bodies that were piled inside. "They're making bets on who'll win."

Finally, we entered a huge room that had a ring in the center of the floor. People were lined up, and there weren't any chairs in sight.

"Come on." She took my hand so we didn't get parted in the crowd.

I wasn't quite sure how she did it, but we wound up in the front, and the two guys were already going at it.

One was a tall, thick guy with a scar down his cheek, who was dancing around the hottest guy I'd ever seen.

My eyes landed on Mason as he grabbed the bottom of his shirt and pulled it over his head. Each movement showed the definition in his hard, muscular body as his shirt was pulled over his short, dark hair. He tossed the material on the ground, and his huge-ass paw print became clear on his upper arm.

Done wasting Mason's time, the scarred guy attacked running full-force at him in the center.

"Kick his ass, Mason," Ella yelled next to me.

My eyes immediately went back to the fight as Mason lowered his body so that the other guy would land on his back. Once the guy was positioned the way Mason wanted him, he stood fast, throwing the guy off his back and onto the ground.

"Ow." The guy groaned as he slowly climbed to his feet. Before he was solid on the ground, Mason reared his arm back and punched the guy square in the nose.

Blood splattered as the guy stumbled in our direction. When he was only a few feet away from us, he hit the ground.

The crowd went wild. The screams and chants were so loud my ears rang.

"Hey, are you okay?" Ella's concerned eyes fell on me.

"Yeah." I didn't need to make a scene.

"If you wanna be concerned about anyone, I wouldn't mind the attention." A guy threw his arm around Ella, and he lowered his face to hers. "You're hot."

"Uh... Thanks." She removed his arm from her shoulders and nodded. "But you're drunk, and we know we don't make the best decisions like that. You might wake up in the morning to find out I'm actually toothless and fat."

"Are you making fun of me?" The guy stood straight and glared at her.

This wasn't good. No one was paying attention because they were on a high from the fight Mason had won.

"See, this is what I'm talking about." Ella took a step toward me, trying to gain distance.

While her head was turned, the guy snarled and raised his hand, aiming it directly at her head.

Oh, hell no. Before I thought twice, I lunged and caught his punch midair. I pushed him backward and kneed him in the crotch as he fell back.

He fell to the ground with a large thud.

That's when I realized that the small crowd around us had their eyes on me.

"Hell, yeah." A guy broke out into a grin and stared me up and down.

I turned, ready to take him on too.

"Oh, no." He lifted both hands in the air. "I was just admiring your work."

"Was he about to fucking hit me?" Ella's eyes stayed on the grounded prick.

"What the hell is going on here?" A dark, raspy voice called from behind me.

Butterflies took flight in my stupid-ass stomach. They should know better than to do that.

"Now you come here." Ella stood and placed her arm around my shoulders. "After Elena took care of the problem. Figures."

"First off, you were supposed to come here with Alec, not her." His emerald eyes landed on mine, and he took a quick intake of air. "What the hell is your name again?"

My damn heart took off, and I could smell the wolf on him so thick. His strong musky scent told me more about him than I should know. He was an alpha, and he expected me to cower in his presence. "None of your concern." I lifted my chin, making sure he knew he had no control over me.

"I don't think you realize how this works." His nostrils flared as his nose wrinkled. "Newbies don't get to run the game."

"Well, first off, I'm not interested in this... game." I wasn't sure what he meant by that. "And secondly, I only came this one time for your sister. It has nothing to do with you. In fact, if I knew we were going to talk, I would've kept my ass home." Really, I would've. I didn't know what the hell was going on with me. My wolf was clawing to get out, and I'd never felt this way toward a guy before, much less a wolf. I wondered... *is it possible he's my mate?* In my position, I couldn't take that chance. This was too dangerous. I needed distance and fast, especially before his wolf figured any of it out.

"Damn, she's feisty." Alec grinned at me. "I knew I'd like you when we met earlier today."

"You should be thanking her." Ella nudged Mason's chest with her finger. "She saved me from the asshole who was trying to hit me." Her nose wrinkled, and she rubbed her pointer finger against her thumb. "Yuck. Go wipe off your sweat and put on a shirt."

"That's a good idea." The words were out before I could stop them. "Because you smell horrible." Yeah, good save.

Ella's eyes lit, and a damn huge smile spread across her face. "How often does a girl tell you that other than me?"

"Are you being serious right now?" Mason's jaw clenched, and his nose wrinkled in disgust. "You almost get hit by some asshole and you're more concerned about her wanting me to put a shirt on?"

"Someone needs to take you down a notch." He shouldn't have been talking to her that way. "And she's not upset because I handled it, unlike someone else here." I was being crueler out of fear of what was going on inside me. My wolf, even though suppressed, wanted to be part of a pack and stand by her mate. How badly I wanted it scared me.

"Alec, take the girls home." He nodded his head in my direction, but his eyes stayed focused on the jackass I took down. "I'll take your car and meet you at the house later."

"Yeah, all right." He waved us forward toward the back door. "Let's get going."

The last thing that I wanted was to be told what to do, but I bit back my complaint. Right now, I needed distance and fast. The longer I stayed here, the harder my wolf was forcing our connection. I had to keep it separate for Kassie's, Mona's, and my protection.

"Hey, Elena," Ella called out as I pushed myself through the crowd.

This had been a very bad decision. I shouldn't have been here, I never should've walked through those doors. My parents had told me about mates. If you were lucky enough to have one, destiny had a way of making sure you meet. At the time, I wanted exactly what Mom and Dad had, but since I lost them, I vowed to do everything I could to stay away in case something like this happened. But here I was, desperate to leave, but a part of my heart had already been fractured and left behind.

CHAPTER EIGHT

That Wednesday morning, I almost decided not to go to class. The last thing I wanted was to see Ella after that night, but the longer I put it off, the worse it'd be.

"Hey, are you okay?" Mona turned toward me as I entered the kitchen. "You were moping all day yesterday."

"Yeah." I hadn't told them what happened the other night and planned to keep it that way. They'd lecture me on needing friends and at least being a normal 'human'.

"Well, did you at least have fun?" Her chocolate brown eyes took me in.

"That's part of the problem." I had. But part of being friends was telling your past and your future. Neither one of those were things I needed to share for multiple reasons. One, if I shared my past, people may figure things out; and two, if they figured it out, they could be captured and tortured at some point.

"It's okay to let others in." Mona took a bite of her standard cinnamon raisin bagel and sighed.

"No, they are weaknesses that could be exploited." I wasn't willing to chance risking Mona and Kassie. They were my family now, and I'd be damned if I let anything happen to them. "Besides," I walked over to her and tapped her on the nose. "I've got you and Kassie, I don't need anything else."

She shook her head at me. "You need friends your own age."

"You've been telling me that for a long time." I made my way to the cabinet and grabbed the peanut butter. "I figured you'd give up by now."

"No." She chewed for a moment and swallowed. "It's just I'm hoping you give it a shot. The worst thing that happens is we pick up and move somewhere else."

That was what we did the first couple of years after the wreck. We constantly moved to ensure that no one figured out I was alive. Finally, we settled down here, and I home-schooled through twelfth grade. I had hoped to do online college classes, but Kassie and Mona refused. They said if they were paying for my education, then college was a must.

I grabbed a banana and peeled it. "Look, I'm going to college onsite. I'm holding up my end of the bargain. You should've made friends a requirement too."

"Maybe we'll consider that for next year." Mona winked at me.

"Hussy." I stuck my tongue out at her as I spooned peanut butter all over my banana.

"I've been called worse." She chuckled as she took another large bite of her breakfast.

"All right, I'm out." I grabbed my bag and purse from the coat hanger by the door. "I'll be home later."

"Have a good day." She hollered before the door shut behind me.

As I made my way to the car, I scarfed my breakfast down. I had spent too much time considering whether to show up today or not, so I was running on the minute, which I hated.

———

MY HANDS WERE SWEATY, which was completely ridiculous. I mean it wasn't like Ella and I were dating or something. When I reached the doorway of the classroom, I took a deep breath and stepped in.

Of course, she was already there, sitting in her normal seat. When she saw me, she waved. "Hey, girl."

At least she was acting normal. I wasn't quite sure what to expect after how Mason blew up. The thought that he might forbid her from being my friend had hurt me worse than I cared to admit.

"I had so much fun the other night." Ella turned her body toward me. "Thank you again for protecting me."

"It was nothing." Even though she and her brother didn't look anything alike, my mind couldn't help but think of him. "He was an ass."

"Oh, yeah. Mason told me that he mopped the floor with him a little more after you left." She snorted. "He came home upset because you did most of the ass-kicking."

"He did plenty of it in the..." Oh crap, I probably shouldn't be saying that here. "Gym."

"You're so cute." She shook her head and pulled out her phone. "So, there is another one Saturday night..."

"No." I had to cut her off. "That was a one-time thing."

"Look, my brother was being an ass. I know." She rolled her eyes and sighed. "For some reason, most girls like that. But you're different. There aren't any ulterior motives."

Dammit. I felt bad now. "Look, I'm not trying to be a

jerk, but my life is complicated." That was one way of putting it.

"Girl, mine too." She reached over and touched my arm. "Look, let's just hang out and have fun. We can make a pact not to disclose our secrets."

The problem was I already knew hers. She was a wolf, and they normally stayed within their pack and social circle. She was taking a leap of faith in trying to hang out with me. Most wouldn't like it... like her brother.

"What would Mason say?" He made it clear how he felt about me, and I didn't want to cause issues with her family or inadvertently think of him.

"I don't give a flying fuck what he would say." She held up her phone, which showed a text.

Don't do anything stupid, but make sure she's okay. Let me know.

"Is that from him?" He'd been all grouchy toward me that night. This was a strange twist. Maybe he was messing with me and Ella.

"Uh, yeah." She tapped her finger on her desk. "It's kind of strange. He's actually asking about you."

He had to have some ulterior motive.

"Are you going to tell him?" The less she mentioned me, the better.

"Hell, no. He was an ass to you the other night." She pulled her phone back and put it in her bag. "I just got it out to turn the damn thing on vibrate."

At least she wasn't going to respond. That had to mean something.

"All right." The teacher walked in at the same time as Connor. "Let's get this going."

I was just relieved that I didn't have to deal with Connor this morning, too.

ELLA LEARNED how I operated because as soon as I began packing up, so did she. Right at the cut-off time, I stood and headed straight for the door.

By now, the professor no longer bothered trying to stop me.

"Hey, let's get our caffeine fix on." She caught up to me in the hall. "My treat. I should compensate you for dealing with my weird-ass family."

"Are we going to the usual place?" I had a feeling she was going to rope me in for the student center.

"I'm missing the blonde roast." She gave a small pout before a smile spread across her face. "Can we go back to the student center?"

"Fine." *She'd better appreciate how much I love her.* "But know this is yet another sacrifice I've made for you."

"I'm totally worth it." She bumped her shoulder into mine. "And you'll survive. You're a big girl now."

We strolled to the student center in silence and went straight to the coffee.

Within minutes, we were both walking out with our special coffee that I was beginning to love.

"Let's go sit..." Her voice trailed off, and she paused.

"What's wrong?" I followed her eyes, and there stood Mason with Alec at the same table as the other day.

"Why the hell is he here?" Her shoulders slumped, and she turned her head toward me. "I'm sorry."

"Let's just go the opposite way." Maybe he hadn't seen us. A girl could hope.

"Yeah, okay."

As we turned to head back outside, his voice stopped me in my tracks. "Ella."

"Shit." She spun on her heel back toward him. "Don't come over here and be an ass again."

"I'm not." He lifted both hands in surrender. "I just wanted to check on... I mean apologize to her." His eyes were nearly my undoing. "Look, I'm sorry about the other night. There was a lot going on, but I should've been nicer to you. I mean, you protected my sister when I couldn't."

"Wait..." She raised a hand and placed it on his forehead. "You apologized. Are you sick or something? Your forehead doesn't feel warm."

"I'm in agreement with her." Alec punched him in the arm. "You've done a lot of shitty things—like sleep with girls and tell them they're worthless right after."

This wasn't what I needed. Him being nice to me would only make this harder. "It's fine. Don't apologize or be nice. Just leave me the hell alone, and everything will be fine."

"Oh, damn." Alec burst into laughter. "I don't think you've ever been turned down by a girl."

"He wasn't asking me for anything." I needed to get away and fast. "Look, Ella, I've got somewhere I need to be. I'll see you Friday."

"But..." Her bottom lip stuck out, and she glared at her brother. "Why are you here? You should be getting settled in for your next class."

Right when I turned to move, she reached over and grabbed my arm. "You aren't getting out of here that easily."

"If she wants to go, then let her go." Mason huffed and shook his head. "I should've known better than to try to be nice to you."

"Yeah, you should've." There was something about him that irritated the hell out of me. I wasn't sure if it was his cocky-ass attitude or that he was a great brother.

Either option didn't bode well for me. "I only came to that fight for your sister. It had absolutely nothing to do with you."

"Well, maybe my sister shouldn't be inviting other people." He crossed his arms and looked down his nose at me.

"If you have such a problem with me being there, why is it okay for her?" I refused to back down.

"It's none of your business." His breathing was ragged, and his nostrils flared.

At this point, I wasn't sure if I was angry, turned on, or both. I wanted to push him down and work all of this sexual frustration between us out so I could move on. "If she invites me again, I'll be damned glad to go."

"I think she might be able to take him," Alec whispered to Ella. "How is this possible?"

"No clue, but I fucking love it." She didn't bother to whisper her response. "I told you there was something about her."

"We don't need you encouraging her." Mason talked to his sister, but his gaze stayed on me. "Sometimes it's best to stay with our own kind."

Even though he hadn't expected me to know what he meant, the message was loud and clear to Ella. I wasn't a wolf, so stay away. "Are you trying to insult me here? What exactly do you think I am?" If he was going to make covert comments, I was going to call him out.

"That's none of your business." A vein popped out between his eyebrows that somehow made him look more attractive.

My wolf was fighting to push forward, desperate to be with him, and this was the first time I had to push back this hard. "I don't have time for your sick, twisted game." I refused to cower. "If you have something to say about me, just say it. Don't be cryptic."

"Fine." He stepped into my personal space, and my breathing turned ragged.

His eyes darted straight to my lips. "You aren't made for us."

"Stop it, Mason." Ella's voice was almost a desperate plea. "She's my best friend."

He groaned as he touched my cheek and breathed me in. "I need for you to stop hanging around me."

"I'm not hanging around you." I needed to be clear and smack his hand away from my cheek, but I couldn't. My cheek buzzed ever so slightly from his touch. "I'm friends with your sister." I hadn't meant for it to happen, but she tore down my barriers.

"I think we might need to give them some privacy." There was a laugh in Alec's voice.

"No." Mason and I shouted at the same time.

"Okay then." Ella tilted her head, examining both of our body languages. "This is strange."

"This wouldn't be strange at all if you hadn't ignored my fucking text." Mason's voice lowered even more.

"Don't talk to her like that." Everything in my being told me to stay and fight him, but this wasn't the time or place. There was a small group forming, watching our very public disagreement. "Apparently, I'm the problem here, so I'll go."

It took everything in me to turn and walk out the door. I wanted to fight and show him I was more dominant, but that wouldn't accomplish anything other than making a scene and upsetting my wolf more.

As soon as I stepped outside, I took a deep breath, but his earthy scent was still strong as if he was surrounding me.

"Wait." He grabbed my arm and gently tugged me around.

"Look, let's not do this." My heart fluttered as he kept a firm grip, not letting me go.

"You feel it too." He pulled me into him, and my legs refused to resist. "I don't understand what's going on. I'm being a dick, and I'm sorry. I'm not trying to hurt you, but whatever is going on between us can't happen."

"Hey, baby." A tall blonde sashayed over and side-eyed me. "What's going on?"

"Leave me alone, Bridgette." His eyes never left mine.

"Are you being serious right now?" She placed her hands on her hips, making her tank top somehow pull lower. Her cleavage was on display for the whole world to see. "Last night, in my bed, you were very attentive." She smirked at me. "It was the best night of my life."

It stung that he slept with her. Maybe I was just imagining this bond between us.

"It was a mistake." He lifted my chin to meet his eyes. He then turned his head in her direction and glared. "I said leave me the fuck alone."

She huffed and continued to stare as if she couldn't believe he'd just dismissed her.

"Look, obviously you and she need to talk." I tried to keep the jealousy from my voice. I had no reason to feel that way. He wasn't mine. My wolf howled inside, refusing to calm down.

"No, I need to talk to you right now." He turned his back on her and focused on me. "I couldn't get you out of my head, and I fucked up. I don't understand what's going on between us."

Our connection wound tighter as if his words were all it needed to strengthen our bond. He felt it too, but he thought I was human. That could be a good thing. He would think it was just crazy lust. Humans can't mate with shifters. It was physically and mentally impossible. "Me neither, but it's probably best for both of us to keep our distance."

It was so ridiculous to be upset over him sleeping with the girl. Shifters had needs, and he was fighting our bond. I couldn't get mad. I was fighting it too.

He rubbed his hand down his face and groaned.

"I'll make it easier for both of us." I turned around, and it took all my strength to pull my arm from his hand and move my legs. Without turning back, I took off as fast as I could and escaped.

CHAPTER NINE

I wound up skipping first period on Friday, not ready to face Ella and her inevitable questions. The way Mason and I were acting toward each other was asinine.

As I drove to the university, I parked in the overflow section. Both Ella and Mason knew where I normally parked so I had to be cautious. I walked the long way around campus heading to the back door of the building where my eleven o'clock class was. The only way they would find me was if they were specifically sniffing me out.

When I was only a few feet away from the classroom, I caught a whiff of Mason's earthy scent.

Shit, he was near.

Before I could even take another step, he appeared, his eyes locking on me.

'Run' screamed in my mind. I glanced at the door only a few feet away from me. It was the girls' bathroom, so I rushed inside.

I was relieved that there were several other girls inside. He couldn't come in here unless he made a huge-ass scene. I should be safe here, at least for a little while. I walked into the closest stall and took a deep breath. Ugh, the stench of shit filled my nose. I should've known better than to do that in here.

It wasn't long before the other girls left, and I glanced at my phone. Class had started, which meant I wouldn't be safe in here for much longer. Everyone would be in class, and the occupants of the bathroom would be sparse. He could walk in here.

Maybe he'd already left. I could be completely overreacting. I walked out of the stall and headed to the door. I didn't have to get close before his comforting scent hit me.

He was still waiting out there.

There had to be a way out of here. I scanned the room, and a window caught my eye. I rushed over to it and moved to open the window but the damn thing wouldn't budge.

"Elena, you okay in there?" Mason's voice was laced with humor. "Did you eat something bad this morning?"

Great, now he was mocking me too.

Then I realized the problem. I hadn't unlocked the damn thing.

I fixed the problem and lifted once more. The window groaned as it opened, but it finally did.

Maybe I could get out of this unscathed after all.

I chucked my backpack out of it and then sat on the window sill. Thank God. I was home free. As I slid out the rest of the way, I was caught by strong, sexy arms.

"I've gotta say no one woman has ever gone that far out of their way to get away from me." Mason's lips turned upward into a huge-ass grin, and he winked at me. "But catching you in my arms made it all worth it."

His hands were wrapped around my body and felt way too appealing. I had to get out of them now. "If I can't make it any more clear that I don't want to see you, I'm not sure what else I can do." I pushed him hard in the chest, forcing him to release me, and he stumbled a few steps back.

"You're something." His eyes scanned me from head to toe, making my body come alive. He must have smelled my arousal because his smirk somehow grew even bigger.

"I've got to get to class." I grabbed my backpack off the ground and slung it over my shoulder. I turned on my heel, but his hand wrapped around my arm, holding me in place.

"There's no point." He glanced at his watch and smiled. "You're already ten minutes late. You'd be rude to interrupt. Let's go grab a coffee instead."

"No." I couldn't be around him. I had to stay away, for his and Ella's safety. I couldn't let my selfish urges take over. "That's a pass."

"I saved you from getting hurt." He pointed at the window that was only three feet in the air. "So, my reward should be a coffee with you."

I couldn't hold back the laugh. "Really, that's the angle you're going with?"

"Yup, you couldn't be that heartless. I'm Ella's brother after all." He arched an eyebrow as he removed the bag from my shoulder and placed it on his. "Come on. It's just a quick coffee, nothing more. It's not like I'm asking for your hand in marriage or anything."

He was right. I was being a little over the top, and Ella did mean something to me. "Fine, but only a quick coffee."

A triumphant grin filled his face. "That's all I'm asking."

"I can carry my bag though." I reached for it, but he side stepped me and marched toward the student center.

Refusing to be left behind, I hurried and caught up. "Don't you have a class yourself?"

"Yup, but you're worth skipping for." He winked at me as he picked up his pace.

My heart skipped a beat, which reinforced why I needed to stay away.

Within minutes, we were heading into the Starbucks at the student center. He placed an order, and I was stunned when he knew exactly what I wanted.

"How did you know my coffee preference?"

"Ella came home the first day she met you and announced to me and Dad that she found her fated best friend. The fact that you enjoyed the drink as much as her meant that there was no turning back." He chuckled. "She is one for theatrics."

"Oh, I know." That was one of the ways she became so endearing to me.

Soon our drinks were placed on the counter and I grabbed mine. "Thanks for the drink." I moved to get my bag back, but he caught my hand.

"We're supposed to have coffee together." He held on to my hand as he used his free hand to grab his cup. "That includes drinking it."

"Okay." I nodded and took my cup, drinking the entire sixteen ounces in one gulp. It burned my throat, and I hated that I wasn't going to get to enjoy it, but gaining distance was more important. Once it was all drained, I slammed the empty paper cup on the table. "There."

"How's that throat doing? Is it a little raw?" Amusement once again filled his eyes.

"Nope, that's how I prefer to drink them." I held out my hand. "Now, my bag please."

"Well, I wouldn't be a gentleman if I didn't at least walk you to your car." He stared into my eyes as he drained his own drink the same way which I had done mine. "There, we can go now."

I wasn't sure how I would be able to get out of this situation while facing the determined look on his face. "Fine, let's go."

When I turned to head into the overflow parking lot, his laughter stopped me in my tracks. I turned around to face him. "What?"

"You really went out of your way to avoid me." He caught up and took my hand, nudging me forward. "It's kind of cute."

Between his words and touch, I almost felt stripped down. I couldn't have this, and it seemed as if I was encouraging him by avoiding him. I yanked my hand out from his and took a few steps to the side so we weren't walking close to one another.

The rest of the walk was in complete silence, and when my car came into view, I almost cried tears of relief. As soon as we reached the driver's side, I turned and grabbed my bag off his shoulder. "Thanks." I pulled the keys out of my pocket and unlocked the driver door. "I'll see you around."

Before I could climb in, he reached around my waist, turning me to face him. "You sure will." He leaned down and brushed his lips against mine, shocking me to my core.

My wolf howled as she clawed inside me, wanting to be free. "Uh." I pulled back and couldn't prevent myself from licking my lips. He tasted way too good. Like coffee and mint. "Bye." I jumped into the car and shut the door, squealing my tires as I pulled away from the parking spot.

As I LAY in bed later that day, I felt like I'd been run through the wringer. Luckily, Mona and Kassie had gone out, so I wasn't bothered with questions. I'd locked myself in my room and focused on getting a handle on my wolf. She was getting stronger and more out of control the more I was around Mason. I couldn't keep going to the witch more and more frequently.

My phone buzzed on my nightstand, so I picked it up.

Hey - Let's go out and grab something to eat. My brother is getting on my damn nerves, and I need girl time.

So, Mason was at home. It shouldn't give me comfort, but it did.

Sorry, no. I've got to study.

The problem was that I wanted to go out with her. This reinforced the fact that I needed to get distance from both of them.

You're a nerd. No go. Be ready in thirty minutes. If you don't come out, I'll give Connor your address.

No, she wouldn't do that. Would she?

Go hang out with some other friends.

This is your last warning. If you aren't outside of your house when I pull up, be prepared for Connor to show up. I doubt it would take him long to get there.

She fought dirty. But I had a feeling she would follow through. I shouldn't be happy about it, but I was. She was a force to be reckoned with.

Jumping up from the bed, I threw on a pair of jeans and a V-neck, cut-rose patterned shirt. I put on some makeup and brushed the flaming red bush that was my hair. Right at the thirty-minute mark, I was ready and rushing downstairs.

I opened the door and found her sitting on her car's hood with her cell phone out and typing. She arched an eyebrow when she took me in. "You were almost too late."

She had to be bluffing. "You said thirty minutes; it's right on the dot." I hurried over to her and glanced at her phone. I couldn't believe what I saw. She had Connor's number pulled up, and she already halfway typed my home address out. "You bitch."

"No, a bitch would be someone who wouldn't warn you." She hit the backspace and deleted the message. "A friend gives a warning. Now come, let's go." She turned and jumped back into her car.

I wasn't sure whether I should be impressed or pissed off. She had a knack for getting her way. I begrudgingly got into the car and slammed the passenger door shut for emphasis.

"Oh, stop. You aren't mad." She waved me off as she put the car in reverse. "You secretly love it."

It scared me that she wasn't far off with that assessment. I needed to do a better job gaining distance. If something happened to her because of me, I wasn't sure if I could live with myself.

"Anyway." She pulled out onto the main road. "We're heading to one of the bars close to town. They have a live band playing."

"I don't like being in crowds." She was a shifter. She shouldn't like being around loud music either.

"We hang outside." She waved me off. "We can still hear the music, enjoy the atmosphere, but not be around all the crammed in bodies."

That was at least a better alternative. "Fine, but if it's too much we leave. Promise me."

"Okay, okay." She lifted a hand in the air. "Whatever it takes for you to at least try to act like a normal teenager."

Within minutes, we pulled up to a huge bar that had an

open back patio. There were several large groups of people hanging outside, and the music blared.

It took everything I had to climb out of the vehicle. Maybe if I refused to get out, she'd forget about me.

As if she heard my thoughts, she made her way to my door and opened it. "Come on. I swear. Look," she said as she pointed to a section that was clear. "We'll go over there, away from everyone."

I wanted to argue but there was no point. I took a deep breath and climbed from the car. "Remember what you promised."

"Yeah, yeah." She waved me on, and soon we were walking across the wood floor of the patio, and we took a seat in the far corner.

As I scanned the people surrounding us, my eyes landed on the blonde that Mason had slept with. It was almost like a punch in the gut.

"Hey, are you okay?" Ella followed my eyes to Bridgette. "Oh, yeah. She's a slut. She's been harassing Mason. I don't know why he does stupid shit like that."

Honestly, I wanted to drop this conversation. I didn't want to think about him and other women. He could never be mine, and it just hurt too much to hear.

"What can I get you ladies tonight?" a young waitress, who couldn't be much older than us, approached and asked.

"Could I get a Coke and some cheese sticks please?" My stomach growled as if telling me it wasn't enough. "And a bacon cheeseburger, medium rare?"

"Sure." She smiled at me and then gazed at Ella. "Oh, a burger sounds good. Let me have the same as her with a large onion rings, my own order of cheese sticks, and some hot wings."

"Uh... sure." The girl glanced at Ella. "Are you expecting more people?"

"Nope, just the two of us." Ella smiled and tilted her head. "I just really enjoy eating."

"Now that's not an understatement." A familiar voice called from across the patio. The wind picked up, blowing his earthy scent in my direction. "But don't worry, she'll share some with her brother." Mason crossed the floor to us, smiling at me, while Alec followed right behind him.

My heart took off when our eyes met.

"Dude, you know she won't share food." Alec laughed loud.

Bridgette's head jerked in our direction, and her eyes landed on Mason. "Oh, hey." A huge smile crossed her face as she ran over and wrapped her arm around his. "I'm over here. I thought you said you couldn't make it."

"I can't." Mason disentangled himself from her. "I'm busy."

The fact that he was blowing her off shouldn't make me happy, but it did. I needed to get out of here. "Ella, I thought it was just us two."

"It was supposed to be, I swear. He was supposed to have a fight tonight." She placed a hand on the table and pointed at Mason accusingly. "How the hell did you know where I was? Did you follow me?"

"It's a Friday night, and I was afraid my sister might get in trouble, so I pushed the fight till tomorrow." He shrugged and turned his back on Bridgette as he moved around the table and took the empty chair that was sitting against the wall, between Ella and me, so Bridgette couldn't join him. As he sat, he scooted the chair closer to me. "Tell her, Alec."

"Uh... yeah." Alec's eyes darted at me but then focused

on Ella. "So... add a burger to that order for me, too, please." He glanced at the waitress.

"Yeah, sure." The girl hurried off, leaving us alone with an angry, scorned lover.

"Are you being serious right now?" Bridgette leaned over the table, placing her girls on full display for Mason. "I invited you here, and you're now turning me down."

"Yup, that's exactly right." Mason pointed over to the group that was standing around across the patio. "You're pretty enough. Someone else will take you home tonight."

Her mouth dropped open, and she blinked a few times before storming off in the direction of her friends.

"You know what?" I needed to leave. His scent was making me dizzy, and my body betrayed me by leaning in his direction of its own accord, in an effort to be closer to him. "I think it's time to go."

"But we just got here." Ella whined.

"Maybe we should sit over there and give them their girl time." Alec winced as he waited for Mason's response.

"Hell, no. I want to be here." Mason's eyes stared right at me.

"You're being weird." Ella arched her eyebrow at her brother. "Which is really saying something about you. I mean you're crossing over a line of strangeness right now."

"We can talk about it later." Mason's hand brushed my leg under the table, making my breath catch.

"I need to go to the bathroom." I jumped to my feet and rushed off in the direction of the restaurant. At this point, I'd rather take my chances with the loud music and a crowd.

As I pushed past a group of guys, one of them reached out and snagged me by my waist.

"Hey there, gorgeous." His words were slurred, and he

was openly gaping at my breasts. "Where do you think you're going?"

"Hands off." Mason's dark, chilling voice broke through the loud music as he appeared, glaring at the man. "She's not yours."

The look on his face and his words implying I might belong to someone... to him... turned me on so damn much.

"Whoa." The guy's eyes widen as he took in Mason and dropped his hand from my waist immediately. "I didn't know. You're one damn lucky man."

"Damn right I am."

Needing distance, I turned and rushed to the bathroom. Right when I got into the small hall that led there, a strong, warm hand touched my shoulder, gently turning me around.

"I can't let you go in there. Remember what happened last time." He stepped close to me, his eyes going straight to my lips.

"What are you doing here?" Every time I tried to run, he appeared.

"You know why." He reached up and brushed a piece of my hair behind my ear. "I can't get you out of my mind."

"Try harder." I had to be strong.

"The problem is I know you are attracted to me, too." He took a step closer to me, making me dizzy. Our chests were almost touching.

In other words, he could smell my arousal. Scent is something that no one can fake. "We're not right for one another." He had to see that this couldn't last.

"Then why does it feel like we are?" He brushed his chest against mine, and I turned, attempting to move around him, but instead, he pushed my back against the wall and trapped me within his arms.

I'd never been this turned on before. If I didn't get my head on straight, I could wind up throwing caution to the wind and having a go with him right here and now.

"Dammit, you're killing me." He groaned as he leaned down, brushing his lips against mine once more.

I gasped as my body reacted, and I found myself licking his lips, tasting him. My wolf howled in approval and began to push to get free of me.

No, this can't happen. I pushed him off of me so hard he flew into the other wall, and I ran back through the restaurant to Ella.

Her hazel eyes landed on me, and she stood. Understanding seemed to flicker in her eyes when she must have noticed Mason running to catch up to me. "All right, let's go."

Thank God I wouldn't have to argue with her.

"What? No." Mason almost yelled the words across the room.

It was so loud that Bridgette's little group turned their attention to us, and Bridgette herself began to grin.

She planned on helping distract Mason from his thoughts of me like she had the other night. It pissed me off even though I had no right to be mad. However, my wolf had other ideas as she struggled to break free from her cage.

"I don't know what the hell is up with you, but we'll talk about this at home." Ella glared at her brother and grabbed my arm, tugging me toward the car.

"Elena, wait." There was a pleading undercurrent in his tone.

"Look, you can forget about me the way you did the other night." I didn't mean to be cruel, but I was hurt, and my wolf had almost gotten free. "She's over there, waiting for you anyway." I pointed at blondie who had bigger jugs than brains.

Something flashed across Mason's face before it set back into the cruel demeanor he had when we first met. "Maybe I will."

"Have fun with that." I turned on my heel and headed to the car, slamming the door behind me.

Ella stood out there and chewed Mason out before climbing into the driver's seat and pulling away.

The entire ride back was in silence.

When she pulled up at my house, she put the car in PARK and glanced at me. "I don't know what to say besides sorry. He's never acted like this before, and I don't know what's going on. I'd hoped to have a fun night with you, but instead, I feel like I messed up."

"No, you didn't." I smiled despite the tears that burned my eyes. He was probably taking Bridgette right now in the back seat of his car. "It's okay. I'll see you Monday." I got out of the car and headed straight to bed.

So HERE I WAS, Saturday night in my room, watching television. Today would've been a work day for me, but when Mona and Kassie found out about the vampire who'd been hanging around work, they pretty much decided for me that I'd better call in sick this weekend or they would show up and make a scene. They wanted me to stay away to see if that would discourage him.

For the first time in my life, I didn't want to be home, but I refused to do anything I'd regret.

Our doorbell rang, startling me from my internal

thoughts. Great, they must have ordered a pizza. I was starving.

I jumped off the bed and opened my door. It didn't smell like food yet, but they probably hadn't brought it in. I ran down the steps and stopped short when I saw him.

"Mason?"

His gaze landed on me. "Hey, sorry to come over unannounced, but I figured you wouldn't talk to me otherwise."

"You got that right." Kassie chuckled and arched an eyebrow at me. "She's a pistol." Kassie tilted her head up, gazing at me. "You hadn't mentioned you had made some *friends*."

She meant hot guys. I wasn't dumb. "Well, it's because no one should know where we live." I crossed my arms and leaned against the wall. "Stalker much?"

"Please ignore her." Mona waved him in. "Come in and visit. She has poor manners. I had thought we raised her better than that."

"Well, in all fairness, I deserve it." He entered the house and went straight to the couch. "I've been a jerk to her."

"So, you're the reason why she came in all in a panic last night." Kassie punched Mona in the shoulder. "We should've known it was due to a guy."

"Will you two be quiet?" They were purposely embarrassing me and encouraging him. "Why don't we go talk outside?" I made my way down the rest of the stairs and headed toward the kitchen.

His footsteps followed mine as I walked out the back door.

When he stepped outside, he laughed. "No wonder you kicked that guy's ass." His eyes were on our little training station.

"Uh... yeah." Damn him. His voice caused a shiver. "So

what do you want to say? I figured we said everything yesterday and that you had to make up with blondie." It hurt to say the words, but I prevented myself from flinching. I had to get used to the idea of him with someone else.

"Who? Bridgette?" His focus landed back on me. "She and I are nothing. I told you I fucked up and I didn't sleep with her last night. You hurt me, so I lashed out in retaliation. I'm sorry."

"You don't have to explain yourself to me." He needed to go, but I wasn't sure how that was possible. He came to my house, and if I went back to my room, there was no telling what Mona and Kassie would do.

"Yeah, I do." He huffed and scratched the top of his head. "Can we sit down for a minute?" He pointed to the two plastic chairs that were on the back porch.

"Okay." I was going to ask how he found me, but we both knew that answer. Ella was getting yelled at as soon as I saw her. "I thought you had a fight tonight.'

"I do." He huffed and gave me a small grin. "This is fucking ridiculous."

"Then feel free to leave." I waved him on. "You found me, not the other way around."

"That's not what I meant." He rubbed a hand down his face. "Damn, you're impossible."

"Sorry if I'm not one of the girls throwing themselves at your feet." I would never be that for him or anyone. I was my own person and strong enough to make it on my own.

"I'm not, but damn, you're making me work for it." He sighed. "Look, my life is... complicated. I'm not ready to tell you why, but there is a very good reason for me to try to stay away from you. However, Wednesday when Bridgette said what she did... the pain on your face..." He ran his hand through his short hair and growled. "It made me realize that I never wanted to make you look that way again."

He was shattering every wall I'd ever put in place with this one conversation. "This could lead to both of us getting hurt." I had to warn him just like he had me.

"You've got some dark secret that you don't want to share with me either?" He laughed until he looked at the expression on my face. "Oh, hell, you do."

"It's something that I don't tell anyone." He deserved to know it had nothing to do with him.

"So Ella doesn't know either?" His forehead creased, and he frowned.

"The only two people who know are in that house." I pointed in the direction of Kassie and Mona. "And the only reason they know is because they were there."

"We can try to keep fighting this between us, but I don't think we're making much ground." He sighed and tentatively held his hand out for mine. "I know being a jackass to you has been making me sick."

Yeah, it wasn't fun for me either. "I don't know what the right answer is."

"How about we just start with this?" He took a deep breath and gently placed my hand in his. "Will you please come to my fight tonight?"

"What?" That was probably the last thing I expected him to say. "Are you serious?"

"Yeah, I am." He squeezed my hand ever so gently. "I haven't been able to get you out of my head for weeks now. I need you to be there for me and Ella."

"You and Ella?" Crap, his sister was going to be pissed. She thrived on the fact that I wasn't interested in him. "She won't like this."

"She knows what's going on." He licked his bottom lip and sighed. "I got her permission before coming here."

"And she's okay with this?" I wasn't, but our bond had already kicked in. The buzzing was stronger now with our joined hands. Even though we both hadn't meant to kick start it, fate was intervening once again.

"If you don't come tonight, I'm going to get my ass kicked. Having you near me helps me stay focused." He snorted and shook his head. "All these years, and you just waltzed in and turned my life upside down."

"It wasn't on purpose." I'd rather we hadn't met either. It would make things easier on both of us.

"Oh, I know." He met my gaze. "And you protected my sister way better than Alec ever could. Please come so both Ella and I make it out in one piece."

The next words that I spoke were going to change my life forever. I knew better. I'd been fighting this hard, but ''yes'' fell from my lips. Our bond somehow had already begun forming. It was too late to turn back. One night couldn't hurt. "Just let me go change real fast."

"I'll be waiting in the car." He grinned at me, which made my breath catch.

I headed back into the house, already regretting my decision. Not only was it a piss-poor one, but I would never hear the end of it from my guardians. It was strange, but that was how I thought about them though they weren't a couple. They were straight and had more action in a day than I had my entire life. But they refused to settle down with anyone because of me, which made me feel more damn guilty.

"So who was that?" I hadn't even taken a step into the den before Kassie was already asking questions.

"The brother of one of my friends." I cringed when I said the last word.

"Friend?" Mona closed her eyes and lifted her head toward the ceiling. "Hallelujah."

"See, this makes me want to take my decision back." Even though I hadn't meant for it to happen, she had become a friend.

"No, honey." Kassie gave me a sad smile. "We're thrilled that you have them, and they're wolves. You need to be around your people."

"They're not my people." I wasn't *Queen*. I wished they'd stopped talking to me like I was. "I'm a human."

"Honey, humans don't have to go see a witch every few weeks." Mona frowned and sighed. "In fact, they avoid them. You actively seek one out."

"Just go have fun." Kassie gave Mona a warning gaze. "We'll stop teasing you. Anyway, Mona and I were thinking about going to the bar down the street and finding a couple of good lays."

"Ew." I felt like they were my parents, so I didn't want to think of them like that. Yes, I may have been an adult, but I hadn't matured that much. "Please stop."

"We're grown women who have needs too." Mona snorted, getting a kick out of my reaction.

"On that note, I'm glad I decided to go." I shook my head and bounded up the stairs.

I looked in the mirror and figured my yoga pants and shirt weren't going to make the cut, so I began scavenging my closet. I found a pair of skinny jeans and a low-cut floral top that tied in the front. It was comfortable but low cut enough to where I wouldn't stand out as a prude or a slut.

Running a brush through my long red hair, I glanced in the mirror. My hair always made me stand out, but I refused to dye it. It hurt to see my reflection; it was easy to tell who my parents were once the connection was made. I grabbed my makeup and quickly put it on before I began over-thinking everything.

I took one last look in the mirror. My eyeliner brought out the blue more, and my lip gloss emphasized my full lips. Taking a shaky breath, I turned and marched out of the house before either Mona or Kassie could say anything else.

As I stepped outside, I stopped in my tracks.

Mason leaned against the driver's side door of his car, looking fine as hell. His eyes scanned over me. A small grin spread across his face. "You look incredible."

"Uh..." I glanced at the ground and bit my bottom lip. I'd received compliments like those fairly often, but they were usually by drunken idiots or guys who wanted to get into my pants. "Thanks." I forced my head up and stared at his eyes. "Should I drive my car too?"

"Well, I asked if you'd come to my fight tonight." He tilted his head and pointed at his car. "I wouldn't have stayed here if I didn't want to take you myself."

"It's really no problem." I didn't want him to feel as if he was obligated to me. We may have been mates, but that didn't mean I wanted to control his life. "It's fine. You'll want to go out with your friends or something afterward."

"Actually, no." He chuckled hard. "I want to hang out with you."

My heart sped up at all the implications that statement could mean. "We need to take this slow. Maybe this is a bad idea." I began to turn around when he jogged over to me and took my hand. It was definitely a bad idea.

"I gotta admit I'm not used to working for this." He threaded his fingers through mine.

"But I'm not asking you to." My breath hitched, causing

the words to come out as just a whisper, but the smile in his eyes told me he heard.

"Doesn't mean I don't want to." He lifted his free hand and tucked a piece of my hair behind my ear. "We can take this as slow or fast as you want."

"But Brid--"

"Please don't say her name again." He winced and shook his head. "Let me be clear. From this point on, there won't be anyone but you." He winked at me. "Let's just see how this goes."

"You're playing dirty." He knew what he was doing.

"Whatever it takes to get you in the car." He tugged on my hand and took a few steps backward toward his car.

"So total exclusivity?" I sounded kind of childish, but we were already in too deep to turn this around. "For both of us? This seems a little too sudden. Everyone knows you're a womanizer." I had to remember that. He would be fine without me. A lot better off than with me.

"I promise. And those days are far behind me."

"Let's not get ahead of ourselves." We needed to stop talking about it, and now. "Let's go." I started to walk around his car when his hand pulled me to a stop to face him again.

"Where do you think you're going?"

Was he playing games now? It would be best if he were. "What?"

"It's only proper if I open your door." He strolled over to the car and opened the passenger door. "You were about to jump in before I could do this."

My heart wanted to burst from my chest. "No, I've got it." I strode over and pushed him aside as I got into the car. As soon as I was settled, he shut the door before I could and walked around to his side.

I had to get my act together and calm my ass down. As he slid into the seat beside me, his earthy scent filled my nose. He smelled like home.

He started the car and looked in his rearview mirror. He had a Mazda that wasn't much bigger than my Civic and had to be at least five years older, but it was kept in good condition.

"I honestly wasn't sure if you would say yes." He put the car into DRIVE and pulled onto the road.

"Technically, I didn't say yes." I had to make sure I didn't do anything to confuse him. We were both going to make this harder, but maybe I could enjoy one night with him before I pushed him away completely.

"Really? You're going to keep fighting this?" A smile tugged at the corner of his mouth.

"Am I that hard to read?" At least I wasn't showing all my feelings like I'd been afraid I did. So maybe I had more composure than I realized.

"Yeah, you are." He frowned and shook his head. "I don't like it."

I wasn't even going to expand on that one.

"Where are we going?" I needed to change the subject and fast.

"I thought we'd grab something to eat first." He slowed down at a pizza place. "Your stomach has been growling ever since we went outside."

"But you'll be late to your fight." I glanced at the time and saw that it was already six-thirty. I hadn't planned for this. I was only supposed to ride with him to the fight and back. No eating, no spending intimate time together. I definitely would've said no if I knew about this.

"Not at all." He pulled into a parking spot and turned

off his car. "It starts at eight, so we have plenty of time to get a pizza."

"Okay." That sounded good, and I was already in his car. If I jumped out and ran home, it would probably raise more questions and intrigue him even more, so I was stuck with my decision. The good thing was that I'd had my mind set on pizza ever since he rang my doorbell. "But remember, this is just as friends."

"Yup. Totally exclusive friends." He saluted me. "Got it." He jumped out of the car and sprinted to my side.

He looked fucking ridiculous but so damn sexy at the same time. He was going to be my undoing.

"Here you go." He opened the door and held his hand out for me to take it.

I hadn't expected that, so of course, I reached out and placed my hand in his. The buzzing was now a pleasurable shock that sprang to life, and my wolf howled inside.

His breath caught as I stood on my own two legs.

"No fucking way." He ran his free hand through his hair. "How is this possible?"

"What?" I forced my expression to remain indifferent and took a deep breath, trying to prevent my heart from racing. Not only was he confused since he thought I was a human, but this bond between us was escalating with little to no encouragement between us. This wasn't how it was supposed to work, so what the hell was going on?

CHAPTER TEN

His eyes landed on my lips as the electricity increased the longer we touched. He leaned his head down and breathed in my scent.

Somehow, our bond had started, and I had no clue how. Mom had always said it began from the first kiss that the couple shared. Did last night already start this? "Come on. We need to go." I slipped away from him and tried to get him to release my hand.

Instead, he held my hand tighter. "Nice try. Let's get you fed. I have a feeling you're not very fun when you're hangry."

"Maybe you're pushing your shortcomings on me." It was so scary how easy this all felt. I knew I had to pull back, but I wasn't sure how to do it right now.

"Nah, I have a feeling I'd have a hard time finding anything wrong with you." He opened the door to the restaurant that seemed to be, once again, full of college kids.

"Is that what you say to all your dates?" I wanted to slap myself. I'd only encouraged him.

"Date, huh?" He arched an eyebrow.

"Uh... I meant..." He placed a finger over my lips, causing our connection to spring to life.

"No, I like that." He scanned my face and smiled. "Don't freak out. Just go with the flow, okay?"

"Okay." I was being ridiculous. We'd just agreed to do this. "Then it's a one-time friendly date."

"Wow." He chuckled. "I've never been so ecstatic to hear those words before."

"Mason." A girl with long black hair ruined our bubble. She wore a low cut top that left little to the imagination and skin-tight shorts. She straightened her shoulders, emphasizing her boobs, and tossed a piece of hair over her shoulder. "Hey. We've got a table over here." She pointed over to a group that included two other girls along with Ella and Alec.

It was foolish, but I kind of thought he was taking me somewhere so we could be alone. This was better though. The less alone time we had, the better. It might at least slow down whatever tension was building between us, and I could get my head on straight.

"Oh." He glanced over and waved at the group. "I didn't realize you were going to be here."

When Ella's eyes landed on me, her face lit up. "Elena." She jumped out of her seat and hurried over to us. "What are you doing here?"

"It's fine." I took a step back. "I'll just head back home. It's no biggie."

"No." Both Mason and Ella said at the same time.

Ella's eyes went to mine and Mason's joined hands. "You didn't know we were going to be here."

When I tried to let go of his hand, he held on tight.

"Obviously, I didn't, or we wouldn't be here." Mason huffed and glanced back at me.

"You were trying to take her somewhere, just you and her?" The dark-haired girl jerked back. "I thought you didn't date."

"It changed today, Meredith." Mason glared at the girl and moved to stand slightly in front of me. "She's officially my girlfriend, so your claws stay hidden. Got it?"

Whoa. This just accelerated, but I couldn't bring my damn mouth to open and correct him. I didn't want her to think she had a chance with him. This was a fucking awful idea.

"Humph." She cut her amber eyes to me. "Don't get too excited. He'll be crawling into my bed before it's all over."

"No, I won't be." He lifted his chin and growled. "And don't talk to her that way again."

"Maybe instead of just opening your legs whenever a guy gives you attention, you could develop a good personality." Ella crossed her arms and stared the girl down. "I mean you should at least try to have one redeeming quality."

I loved that girl so fucking much, but I refused to be talked down to. "Usually the type who threaten are over-compensating for something." I turned and fixed my gaze on hers. "Do you have daddy issues or something?"

Meredith jerked back as if she was slapped. "You…"

"It's best if you shut the hell up." Mason scowled at her. "The next words you say will make me come unglued, and we're around…" He glanced at me and cleared his throat, "a lot of people."

"Be a good girl, and let my brother have his date." Ella winked at me and turned on her heel. "Besides, I like them together."

Meredith glared at me as she slammed right into my shoulder in an attempt to knock me aside.

I stood tall and shoved back into her too. I wasn't going to let someone treat me like that. If I did, things were only going to get worse.

She stumbled and fell to the ground with a loud thud. "You bitch."

Mason lurched forward, but I tugged him back.

"The number-one rule of taking on someone is making sure you can win." I squatted so I was close to eye level with her. "Don't fuck with me."

"Girl, I love you so much." Ella laughed so hard she clutched her side. "That's been a long time coming."

"Come on." Mason stepped around Meredith, making the situation that much more comical. "There's an open table over here."

Not wanting to be a complete ass, I gave her a wider berth, but when I glanced at her one more time, something like respect reflected in her eyes.

Yeah, I wasn't going to analyze that one. I followed after him as he made his way to a table that was across the restaurant in the corner.

When he reached the table, he pulled out the chair for me. "I'm sorry about that."

"It's fine." I sat, and he stepped over to his chair. "I mean we're just friends after all."

"No, it's not, and we both know better, no matter how desperate you are to not admit it." He ran his hands through his short hair. "I'm going to be honest. I've never dated someone."

"You don't say?" He acted like that was brand new information.

"Touché." He leaned back in his seat as the waitress appeared. "Hi, do you guys know what you want?"

My stomach growled loudly once more. "Can I get a large pizza with all the meats?" Oh crap, I was used to being alone. "I mean if that's okay with you."

"Make it two." He tapped the table with his finger. "And I'll take a Coke."

"Water for me, please." I gazed out the window, not quite sure what to say next.

"So, you've got two moms?" He leaned back in his seat and got comfortable.

"Yeah, something like that." Eventually, I would have to tell him my story, but it wasn't going to be tonight. So I gave him the shortened version. "My parents died young, and Kassie and Mona raised me."

"Oh, I'm sorry." He winced and scratched the back of his neck with his hand. "I didn't realize."

"Don't." Flashes from that day filtered through my head. I couldn't break down here. "I... don't want to talk about it."

"Yeah, okay." He nodded his head and licked his bottom lip. "Well, they sure seem nice. I mean this is a stupid question, but do you know them well?"

Ah, he was fishing. "Of course. I've lived with them every day for the past twelve years. Why would you ask that?" He was trying to figure out how much I knew about wolves.

"No reason." He cleared his throat and pursed his lips to the side. "You're enjoying making me squirm."

"What?" I mashed my lips together, trying to hide my laugh. "No." But it slipped through anyway.

"You sneak." He laughed and reached over the table,

taking my hand in his. The electricity sprung to life, and my wolf howled louder in my head.

I yanked my hand back, but the place he had touched still tingled. I was playing a dangerous game, and I could only hope that I knew what I was doing.

WE ROLLED up to the gym about a quarter till fight time.

"Are you sure we aren't late?" I'd been stressing the entire time. "I don't want you to get in trouble."

"Aw, that's cute." He parked the car and turned to face me. "I'll be fine. Come on; let's head inside so I can make sure you and Ella are settled before my fight."

I jumped out of the car before he had a chance to open my door. Boundaries. I needed to have boundaries. "They should already be in there. They left before we did."

"Alec likes to get here early. That's all." We strolled through the parking lot toward the building. "I'm surprised that you haven't asked me why I do this yet." He caught up to me and took my hand.

I tried releasing my hand from his grasp, but once again he held it firmly in his. "Ella already told me about your mom." I hoped he was okay with the fact that she had.

"Of course she did." He shook his head and squeezed my hand. "It's going to take some getting used to."

"What?"

"You being tight with my sister." He tugged me closer and released my hand, wrapping his arm around my waist. "It's actually really nice. I'd always hoped that my ma... girl-friend got along with her."

He almost slipped with the *mate* word. I should have called him out on it, but I wasn't prepared for that conversation quite yet. When I attempted to slip out of his hold, he wouldn't let me budge. The problem was I loved that he wouldn't. My walls were already breaking down faster than I ever thought possible. The bond was forcing itself, and my will to stay away was crumbling.

"Is your dad out of the picture?" It hurt to think that he had to put the pressure all on his shoulders.

"Nope, but he's got a demanding job, so he can't make extra money." When we reached the door, he jogged in front and opened it for me. "So I'm doing this until we have enough for the right person to heal her."

I thought about pushing him through the door and following through it after him, but I couldn't find the strength to be an ass. "Sounds like your dad has a big job." I figured his dad must be the alpha of their pack. If so, why wouldn't my uncle help him?

"He does." He placed his hand on the small of my back as I walked through. "He takes care of a lot of people and is trying to do the best he can. I'm just helping out in the background."

"So, in other words, he doesn't know you're doing this." He and I were more alike than I realized.

"Yup, and it's going to stay that way." He kept his hand secured on me as we headed toward the crowd.

This time, I was at the mercy of his touch.

Unlike last time when Ella and I had to push our way to the front, the crowd parted for Mason.

"Hey, man." A guy held up a wad full of one hundred-dollar bills. "I'm staking my retirement money on you. Make me proud."

Mason nodded at him and kept moving.

It wasn't long before we were in the front where the fighting ring was. "Break a leg." I turned to smile at him.

"Nope, you're going over there with me." He pointed to the corner of the ring where Alec had been sitting the other night.

"But there is only one chair." The last thing I wanted was to kick his friend out of his seat.

"I'll take care of it." He took my hand in his and tugged me over to the corner.

"Hey, man." Alec appeared from the back room and punched Mason in the shoulder. "Are you ready?"

"Yup." Mason strolled into the back room and came out with two additional chairs. "Where's Ella?"

"Oh, she's in the bathroom." He nodded to the door against the far wall.

"The rest of them?" Mason set the other chairs on the ground next to his side of the ring.

"They're over there doing some betting." Alec's eyes landed on me. "And if they were going to say something to your parents, they would've by now."

"Yeah, but that still makes me nervous." Mason looped his finger through one of my belt loops and tugged me toward him.

The door to the women's bathroom opened, and Ella came marching out. "You guys are so freaking cute."

I wasn't sure how to respond. All I knew was if I didn't get out of here soon, my will to stay away would dissolve, and my defenses would be nonexistent. It already hurt to think about it. Maybe I could sneak out when he got distracted with the fight. I could either run home or call one of my guardians to pick me up.

"She sits in between you two." Mason pointed his thumb at Alec and pinky at Ella. "Make sure she doesn't try to sneak out."

"You think I'd do that?" He had me pegged and ruined my plan with little effort.

"Hell yeah, you would." He grabbed a bag off the ground and turned toward the men's bathroom on the other end of the wall. "I'll be back. If you run off, I know where you live." He winked at me. "I'm going to change real fast."

As he strolled away, I rubbed my eyes and took a steadying breath. Tonight was a whirlwind, and I needed to get my head on straight. I struggled to do that around him.

"If you're worried about me being upset, don't be." Ella quietly clapped her hands. "I never thought he'd settle down, but this is amazing."

"Settling down." That confirmed that he told her about our bond. "We've agreed to take it slow."

She raised a hand. "I have a good feeling about this." She sat on her seat and patted the chair next to her. "Come on and sit down. Shit's about to get real."

I turned around and saw the announcer, or whoever it was, head in our direction. He appeared to be in his twenties and had his long chestnut hair in a man bun. He was also stout, and he wore a tight black shirt and jeans, which accentuated his muscles. "Where the fuck is Mason?"

"He'll be out here in a second." Alec lifted both hands up. "He had to go change."

"He better get his ass out here. It's time." The guy nodded his head at whomever Mason's contender was.

The guy he was fighting was tall and slender, but there was something cruel in his dark eyes. He didn't smell like a shifter but didn't have a human scent either. What the hell was he?

"It's about time that your ass gets here." The man-bun guy growled as his eyes locked on someone behind me.

"Don't get your panties in a wad, Matt." Mason's deep chuckle did tingly things to my insides. "I'm here."

When I turned around, my eyes couldn't get enough of him.

Mason was shirtless once again with his wolf tattoo on display. My eyes traveled down his body to his six-pack, and before my gaze could get lower, Ella snorted.

"You're totally eye-fucking him."

"What?" That hussy just called me out in front of everyone. "No."

"Don't lie." She shook her head with a huge-ass grin on her face. "I mean it's one thing that I'm happy you guys are doing whatever you are, but don't eye-fuck him in front of me."

"Hey." Mason glared at his sister. "She can do anything she wants to me. We don't need to have your permission."

They both were goading me. However, his opponent was staring at me and making me feel a hell of a lot more uncomfortable. "You better get serious." I didn't want Mason to lose after what I learned about his mother.

"You think I might lose?" Mason glanced over to the guy and back at me. "How 'bout this. If I win, I get a kiss goodnight?"

"A kiss? That's what you want?" Those were damn high stakes considering what was going on between us.

"Yes, one hundred percent." He held out his hand to me.

"And if you lose?"

"That's up to you." He stepped in front of me, his eyes holding mine. "What do you want?"

"A night out with Ella." He had control issues when it came to his sister, and now I realized why she acted so smothered. "With you not suddenly appearing or driving us crazy."

"Hell, yeah." Ella pumped her fist in the air. "For the first time, I'm not sure whether I want you to win or not."

"It's time." Matt held the microphone up to his mouth and grinned. "So who's ready for some fighting?"

At that moment, I realized how screwed I was. There was no way I was going to be able to stay away from him or Ella, which meant some hard decisions were going to have to be made.

CHAPTER ELEVEN

A s Matt entered the ring, the crowd went wild. My ears rang with their shouts and catcalls.

"We've got Mason fighting against Kurt."

Both men circled the outside of the ring with their hands in the air.

Ella and I had gotten here later the other day, so I hadn't been able to witness this first-hand.

Of course, Meredith was standing close by, taking Mason in when he passed by her. I couldn't blame her though. He was a force to be reckoned with.

"Let's do this." The guy leaned back and rang a bell. "Let's get this show on the road."

Kurt didn't waste any time as he seemed to flash right in front of Mason and punch him in the face. He hadn't caught Mason off guard, so he was able to block it and kick out his foot toward the guy's stomach.

Once again, the guy's hand was barely visible as he threw multiple punches at Mason.

Holy shit. Kurt had to be a vampire.

Somehow, Mason ducked and threw his body into the

guy's stomach, causing him to stumble in his tracks and fall onto the ground.

As Mason landed on top of him, he rolled off and jumped to his feet. As he went to kick the guy, Kurt grabbed Mason's foot and yanked it out from underneath him. His ass landed with a thud that could probably be heard throughout the whole room.

My gut reaction was to jump in to help. I stood, but Ella grabbed my waist, pulling me back down. "No, you can't go in there. It'll disqualify him."

Within seconds, Kurt ran over and lifted his leg, ready to kick Mason in the face.

Mason groaned in pain as if he was injured, but as Kurt kicked forward, Mason rolled onto his back and swooped the legs right out from under Kurt.

A loud crunch filled my ears as Kurt fell awkwardly on his arm. "Agh."

Not giving any mercy, Mason leaned over and punched the guy in the face repeatedly. Soon, Kurt's eyes rolled into the back of his head.

The loud bell rang again, and Matt ran into the ring and held up Mason's arm. "And once again, Mason wins."

The crowd cheered louder than in the beginning.

I had to restrain myself from jumping all over Mason when he walked down the stairs. He glanced at me and winked. "I can't wait for my prize tonight."

"You're impossible." My stomach seemed to take flight at his words.

"I had extra motivation to win this one." He reached out his hand that was covered in blood, and I took it.

"Uh..." Ella elbowed Mason in the side. "Hello."

His green eyes widened. "Oh, yeah." He jerked his

hand away and grabbed a towel, wiping the remaining blood off. "I'm sorry. I didn't think."

Oh, yeah. Humans were squeamish around blood. "Ew. Gross." But my voice fell flat.

"Come on." Matt patted Mason's shoulder. "Let's go get your winnings so I can clear everyone out of here. The longer they're here, the more likely the cops will get a call."

"So, um." Alec nodded his head in the direction of my hand. "You got some blood there."

"Here," Ella grabbed the towel and threw it at me. "You'll be as good as new."

I caught the towel and took a few steps toward the ring as I wiped off the vampire's blood. I already didn't react like a human, so I needed at least a little space. Hopefully, the rest of the night wouldn't get any worse.

Meredith and two other scantily clad women began talking to Alec and Ella, giving me a break from their attention.

"You smell so familiar." An elegant, deep voice filled my ears.

Shit, could he be part of the vampire clan that the witch was trying to eliminate? I hadn't considered it until now. "What? Are you talking to me?"

Kurt took a few steps toward me as he narrowed his eyes and stared right into mine. "You've been a very naughty girl."

"I have no clue what you're talking about." I needed to go visit the witch and soon. "Sorry, you must have me confused with someone else."

The vampire's eyes glowed ever so slightly. "Why are you working with the witches?"

He was trying to mind control me. That was one of the nice things about being wolf royalty. I was too strong to bend to their power. "Once again. No clue what you're talking about." I turned to escape, but the vampire jumped out of the ring and grabbed my arm.

"Do you think I'm an idiot?" His voice was loud as he stared daggers into mine. "Now, answer my question."

"Whoa." Alec hurried over. "What's going on over here?"

"It doesn't concern you." Kurt jerked me closer to him as he took a deep sniff of me. "What are you?"

"She's a person." Ella loudly laughed. "What else could she be?"

I refused to cower to him. That's what he wanted. I stood straight and met his stare. "Do you actually think I would tell you?"

He hissed, and his canines began to extend.

"Get the fuck away from her." Mason's loud voice and growl seemed to fill the room.

But Kurt acted like no one had spoken to us. "You better be careful." His mouth spread into a large smile. "I'm not always so gentle." His hand clasped my neck, and he began to squeeze.

This asshole had gone too far. With all my strength, I jammed my knee into his crotch, causing him to release his grip on my neck and fall to the ground.

"I guess one person beating the shit out of you wasn't enough." I pretended that I was going to kick at his face, and he reached for my foot that never appeared.

Instead, I dropped with my elbow right on his neck. He went limp immediately.

"Who the hell is that?" Matt's drab olive green eyes scanned me over. "I mean, I knew she was fucking hot, but you didn't tell me she could fight."

Mason shook his head and scowled. "No. No, you're not."

"I don't think that's up to you." Matt jogged over to me and smiled. "You're hot and badass. We could make so much money together. Where did you train?"

"First off, none of your business; and second, I'm not interested." The last thing I needed was any attention on me. I had to stay under the radar. If my uncle somehow caught wind and saw my picture, it would all be over.

"Don't listen to him." Matt waved Mason off. "This is strictly a conversation between you and me."

"My decision has nothing to do with him." I hated narcissistic assholes that tried to manipulate people into doing what they wanted. "So, fuck off."

Matt's face spread into a huge-ass grin. "You say that now, but just wait."

I was done talking to him. "Are you ready to go?" Between the vampire and now this guy, I wanted to get the hell out of here.

"Yup." He captured my hand and tugged me toward the door. "Alec, make sure Ella gets home safe."

"Aren't you going to the bar?" Meredith frowned and stared at my and Mason's joined hands.

"Nope, not interested." He waved at the other two girls. "I'll see you around."

"Bye, Elena." Ella rushed over and gave me a hug. "I'll see you in class Monday."

"Bye."

WE WALKED out into the parking lot, which was pretty much dead. It was kind of eerily quiet now after all of the noise and commotion in the gym.

"That was kind of interesting tonight." Mason chuckled as he held the door open for me.

"What was?" I slid into the seat, hoping he wasn't going to bring up the vampire.

He shut the door and jogged to his side and climbed in. "What did that ... guy say to you?"

Vampire had almost crossed his lips. I felt bad holding back my past, but I had to protect all of us. "Oh, nothing. Rambling about me smelling familiar." If this wasn't confirmation that I had to stay away, I wasn't sure what else would be. Tomorrow, Mason Lockly could no longer exist for me.

His hands tensed on the steering wheel for a second before he started the car. "You don't seem very upset about it."

"Guys say weird things to me all the time." I shrugged. At least I wasn't lying on this one. "You kind of get immune."

"Well, I hate that I wasn't the one to kick his ass again." He pulled us onto the main road heading back toward my house. "You're awfully strong."

I figured this was going to come up. "You kicked his ass better." I cleared my throat and gazed out the window. "Where are we going?"

"I'm taking you home."

For some reason, I hadn't expected that, and I probably should've. Of course, he wanted to go hang out with his friends. It was better this way. "Okay."

"What's wrong?" He glanced at me and reached over the console to intertwine our fingers.

"Oh, nothing." The last thing I wanted was for him to feel obligated to spend time with me. I savored his touch, knowing it would be one of the last ones I would ever experience with him.

"Will your guardians be upset if we chill on the back porch for a little while?" He squeezed my hand comfortingly.

"Guardians?" My breathing increased. "Why would you say that?"

"Because you said they raised you and aren't a couple." He tilted his head and glanced at me. "So that would make them your guardians."

"Right." So many parts of my life were getting crazy. It felt like I couldn't keep up. The longer Mason and Ella spent close to me, the more I'd be putting them in danger. It wasn't right. I had to come clean or leave.

Now that I had made that decision, the drive home seemed twice as fast as normal. I took a deep breath and turned my body toward him. "Do you mind if we stay in the car for a second?" This was it. Even if I had to pull out of the university, I couldn't be around either one of them any longer. They both already found a place in my heart. The more time I spent with them, the more they'd take.

"Of course not." He put the car in PARK and reached over to take my hand. "I'm ready for my prize."

"You aren't leaving yet."

"I never claimed it was a goodbye kiss." His eyes once again flickered to my lips. "And honestly, I can't get it off my mind."

My heart raced as he leaned over the center console. "Wait, I need to tell you something first." I had to somehow make him want to stop.

"Nothing you say will change my mind." His fingertips touched my cheek, ever so gently caressing it.

"But we probably should know certain things before doing this." My wolf and body yearned for his touch, but I didn't want him to regret his decision. I was determined to make him see how wrong this was for all of us.

"We have all the time in the world to learn them." His lips brushed against mine softly at first, causing electricity to course through my body.

Not able to refuse him any longer, I opened my mouth, and my tongue ran along his lips.

He groaned and wrapped his fingers in my hair, opening his mouth and matching my tongue, brush for brush.

My wolf surged forward, and a low growl emanated from my throat. The intensity began to grow between us, and my wolf lashed against my body.

Shit, she was trying to force the change on me. I gasped and jerked back, grabbing my head.

"Elena, what's wrong?" His voice was laced with concern.

"I need Rose." I wasn't ready for my uncle to know about me yet. Not now.

"A flower?" He glanced around outside like he was searching for some kind of blooming plant.

"No, witch." With shaking hands, I grabbed my purse and pulled out the sticky note with her number written on it. "Call her, please. Take me to her." I had meant to make him run away by telling him a lie. But it appeared that the truth would have to do it. He already knew one of my secrets.

He unfolded the paper and grabbed his phone. It wasn't long before she picked up.

"I'm calling for Elena. She's screaming in pain, and she says she needs you now." He paused for a moment and took a deep breath. "We'll be there in ten minutes."

He squealed out of the yard to take me to her.

MY WOLF RAN RAMPANT INSIDE, trying to force the change on me. If she gained it, she knew we'd finally be synced enough for her to have influence.

It took all my focus and energy to keep her in check.

"We're here." Mason's tone was tense, and he turned off the car. "Are you sure we should be here?"

I slowly nodded my head, sweat covering my forehead. I didn't have the energy to say no.

"Okay." He jumped out of the car and opened the passenger door. He picked me up gently, and I laid my head on his chest, listening to his heartbeat.

Luckily, the door was unlocked despite the sign being off. When he stepped inside, he pulled in a quick breath. "Witch."

I was going to have to explain everything when this was all said and done. Maybe he'd keep my secret and leave without a fight. Then again, a part of me hoped the bond would make him want to stay, to at least protect me.

"Put her on the ground." Rose ran into the room with her bowl. She grabbed a dagger from the counter and scrambled the rest of the way to me. "You're almost too late." She dropped to her knees and reached for my hand. "You have to pay the price, or the spell won't work."

"Get that away from her. What the hell?" Mason's voice was laced with warning.

"Each spell requires a sacrifice." The witch ignored him as her eyes stayed on mine. "I'm sorry."

"Do ... it ...." The vampires couldn't be worse than my uncle.

She nodded as she reached over and picked up my hand.

"What the hell. Do not cut her." Mason's voice was more rasp than tone at this point.

"It's not your decision," Rose spoke harshly as she pierced my finger and took a drop of my blood.

My wolf roared more in desperation. She knew what was going to happen.

Rose touched my hand and mouthed the words of the spell.

Magic swirled inside me and slammed my wolf back inside her cage. As soon as her spell was completed, she ran to the back room with my blood.

I took a deep breath and relished the fact that the internal struggle was gone.

"She was close to breaking free." She appeared from the back room and raised an eyebrow. "Are you okay?"

"Yeah." My voice was barely a whisper. The fight between me and my wolf had been tiring. I was exhausted, and it took every ounce of strength to get up from the floor. "But we need to talk."

"I'd have to agree with that statement." Mason leaned against the cash register, staring at me as I remained sitting on the ground.

"Hey, I tried." I wasn't going to take any of his shit over this. I had already decided to come clean before we kissed. He was the one who was going to take the fall on that one. "Don't get mad and grumbly on me. We can talk when we get home." My eyes settled on Rose. "I want to know what you're using my blood for."

"That's none of your concern." She lifted her head and shook it at me. "That breaks our arrangement."

If she thought that was going to work, the bitch had another thing coming.

CHAPTER TWELVE

"That all changed when a fucking vampire recognized my scent." If she thought she could play the innocent card, I knew I'd have to call her bluff now. I only hoped that Mason would stay quiet and ask questions after we left.

"Are you talking about the one I fought tonight?" Mason tilted his head as he processed my words.

"Yeah." I didn't turn my gaze on him. Rather, I kept my eyes on her. "I'm assuming you've got something to do with that."

"What? That shouldn't be possible." She placed her hand on her chest where her heart beat. "I've been diluting your blood and everything."

Mason growled as he crossed his arms.

"Obviously not enough." That had to be why that vampire at work had been stalking me. "Between him and the vampire that keeps visiting my work, I'd say more than one has already figured it out."

"Only a very strong alpha's blood would allow a vampire to distinguish the scent of the blood the way the we've been using it." She pursed her lips and tapped her foot. "Which is impossible in your case seeing as you've never shifted."

A quick intake of breath told me that Mason was piecing it all together. "It doesn't matter if it should be possible or not." He pushed off the counter and moved to stand beside me. "The fact is they are."

"You do realize he's going to cause you to have more of a struggle, right?" Rose arched her eyebrow so high it hid under her bangs. "First off, he has a strong wolf; and second, your two wolves are mates. Your wolf is going to want to come out."

"Do you not think I realize that?" I had been desperate to get here. "The bond is forcing itself on us."

"Have you two been fighting it?" Rose's eyes landed on Mason. "I'm a little jealous that he's yours."

"Focus on those last two words you just said, and stop fucking with us." He wrapped his arm around me. "You better stop using her blood. If something happens to her, there's no telling what could happen to you."

This wasn't good. Why was he protecting me? He should be disgusted and not want to be near me. I needed him to realize the truth and walk away because I didn't have the strength to fight it any longer. I was too weak and tired.

"Are you really threatening me right now?" Rose closed her eyes and shook her head. "After I just helped her."

"I'm not sure that you are helping her if she has vampires hunting her down." Mason's fingers dug into my hip a little.

"And I just gave you more blood." Mona and Kassie had been right. I should've never trusted the hag. Maybe the price was too high. "What are you going to do with it now that you know?"

"We still need it." She huffed and straightened her shoulders. "Those vampires are attacking our covens."

"What for?" I deserved to know now.

"That is official coven business and not something that I can openly discuss with you." She huffed and tapped her foot on the ground. "But you've saved so many lives."

"That's great to know." At this point, why did it matter whether she used my blood again? They were already targeting me. "All right, we've gotta get back before people start worrying about us."

"I'm more than ready." There was an edge to Mason's tone.

He was pissed, and I understood.

"You have my number if you need me." She grinned and motioned toward the door. "I'll lock up after you."

Mason took my hand and almost ran to the door. Granted, he had a good five inches on my five-foot-ten-inch self.

Once we took a step outside, I had expected him to drop my hand, but he didn't. However, we walked in silence straight to his car. He opened the door for me and shut it, climbing inside the car within seconds.

I'd expected a ton of questions, but he remained silent as he drove, heading to God-knew-where. I wanted to ask where, but I was afraid to be the one to speak first. Not that I was scared of him, but I was, instead, terrified of his reaction.

We pulled into a section of town I'd never been to. We turned on a gravel road, and he continued on until we reached a small lake.

He stopped his car and got out.

Needing to figure out his thoughts, I opened the door and climbed out before he could reach my side.

He must have heard because he headed the five feet to the lake.

I followed behind him and stopped a few inches shy of him. I needed him to be the one who broke the silence.

A breeze picked up, blowing a few pieces of hair behind my shoulders. There was a little bit of a chill in the air now that we were getting to the end of September.

"It's strange." He kept his head facing forward, staring off at the lake. "I'm not sure whether I should feel pissed, relieved, or indifferent."

"Indifferent?" That concerned me most of all, but it was what I needed. If he didn't care, he would leave.

"Yeah, because it doesn't matter." He huffed and turned around to face me. "You're it for me. There's no turning back, and now I know you feel it too."

"I do." I bit my bottom lip and ran my hand through my hair. He wasn't doing what I expected him too. He planned to stay, and I wasn't sure that I could fight it any longer. Still, he had to know the truth. What he was getting himself into if he wasn't the one to walk away. It was his call. "I was trying to end things with you before we kissed. There's so much you don't know."

"At least it makes sense now. I thought I was going crazy. A wolf mating with a human is impossible. Now, I learn that you're a wolf shifter who's suppressing her own damn wolf with the help of a witch?" A humorless laugh barked out of him. "Damn, that sounds crazier out loud than it did in my head."

"It does." I blew out my breath. "There are things about me that you don't know."

"Then let me in." He ran his hand over his face and shook his head. "There isn't anything you could tell me that would change how I feel."

"I never meant to get you to bond with me." I had to make sure he realized that it caught me by surprise just like him. "In fact, that's why I was so hostile and tried so hard to avoid being around you. For your safety, you need to walk away from me."

"No. There's no way in hell I'm walking away, and I don't think you manipulated the bond." He rubbed his forehead as if he had a headache. "When the witch asked if we had been fighting it, it made me remember something my grandmother told me."

"Oh, really?" Maybe he had a piece of the puzzle.

"On her deathbed, she told me the true tale of her and my grandfather." He took a step toward me and sighed. "Apparently, she fought the bond, which isn't natural. Because of that, fate took control and began to force their bond to merge until they both were in too deep. We did the same thing."

I should've known better. "The strongest alphas always find their mate, so the bond has to do what it needs, to make them one." There was no way we could go on now. Our souls had begun merging. "I'm sorry."

"Why?" He reached for my hand and intertwined our fingers. "I'm not. Before that day I saw you in the hallway looking for your class, I kind of was just going through the motions."

"Wait. You saw me?" I remembered it was right after I freaked out the first time in the student center with Ella. I had run out, getting to my next class early. That was the first time I saw him, and I didn't have a clue he noticed me.

"Yeah, I was trying to act aloof." He laughed. "You smelled human."

"I believed I could be human." I wished I could say that

I hoped this had never happened, but I couldn't fathom life without him. "I can't shift."

"Why not?" His green eyes sought mine for answers. "Why would you not embrace your animal?"

"What I'm about to tell you, it's something I've never told anyone else before." I couldn't face him. I couldn't watch his reaction. I stepped around him and faced the lake. "I don't want anyone to know about this. Not even Ella, okay?"

"Of course." His voice grew louder as he turned toward me. "Every part of you is safe with me."

That was the problem. I may have been safe from him, but he was most likely not safe because of me. "I told you that my parents died, right?"

"You did."

"But I didn't tell you what caused it and how they died." Memories flashed through my mind, and I took a deep breath, trying to hold back the tears. "I was six years old, and we were at a dinner party. King Adelmo was there for a visit."

"Wait. The top alpha of Europe?" His tone was an octave higher than it usually was.

If I wasn't bearing my soul to him, I would've made fun of him. "Yeah, he was visiting Dad and Mom to talk about something political." A laugh almost slipped out as I thought back at my mom rolling her eyes at me. "But my uncle came over unannounced and told Dad that he needed to talk to him immediately."

I paused a moment to see if he was going to speak, but the only thing I could hear was the ripples of the water from the breeze. "Dad took him to his study while my aunt told Mom that she needed to talk to her." All the details were foggy, but it didn't matter. The outcome was the same. "As we followed my aunt, my uncle's son, Richard took Adelmo to the library. As we walked into the room with my aunt, she turned around with a knife in her hand."

Now, all I could see were the memories. "She went for me first, but Mom somehow managed to kick her at the last second despite the long gown she had been wearing that night. With all the noise, Mona ran into the room and told us to run."

I'd never forget the terror that reflected in Mona's eyes. "Mom and I ran out toward the kitchen when Dad and Kassie showed up. Dad's coat had been ripped from where a knife cut into him. Anyway, long story short, Dad, Mom, Kassie, Mona, and I jumped into one of the vehicles in the garage. Mona and Kassie sat in the back with me with their guns out and ready for whatever might happen."

"Someone followed you." Mason's words weren't a question but a statement.

"Yes, someone did. They ran us off the road, and we rolled toward an embankment and wound up in the water." A tear managed to escape and slide down my cheek. "Mona got me out, and Kassie tried to save them, but they were already dead. Kassie barely escaped before the car exploded, removing any evidence of what happened."

"Why does that story sound so familiar?"

He was a little boy when it happened, so that was probably why it didn't stand out in his mind. "Because it was the day your king died, and soon after, his brother, King Darren, ascended the throne."

"You're the princess who died." His voice was a whisper. "But you're the rightful heir to the throne."

"I don't want it." I finally turned around, surprised to see concern lining his face. "My parents lost their lives because of the crown."

"Oh, baby." He closed the distance between us and wrapped his arms around my waist. "I'm so sorry. No wonder you haven't let anyone close."

"That's why the vampires can recognize the scent of my blood." I buried my face into his chest, sharing the burden with someone for the first time in my life. "I thought since I hadn't allowed my change, my blood would be less potent."

"Your blood is your blood." He kissed my forehead and sighed. "Changing doesn't alter your DNA. It's who you are. Is that why you've been trying not to shift?"

When he said it like that, it made me feel ignorant. "Well, not exactly." I raised my head so I could see his face. "You know how an alpha can feel the members of his pack once everyone goes through their first shift?"

"My father is our alpha, and yes, he's told me."

"The king can feel all of us." It wasn't something that was widely discussed even though it wasn't a secret. "If I shift, he'll know..." My voice broke off.

"That you're alive." He took a deep breath and exhaled. "That makes sense, but I'm worried about what it's doing to you. You couldn't see the way you looked tonight."

"She's been getting stronger." I couldn't believe how supportive he was being. I figured he'd be grossed out or thought I was a coward.

"You do realize that you aren't actually two separate beings, right?" He reached over and pushed a piece of hair behind my ear. "That's probably one reason you're struggling. Your soul is splintering."

Yeah, that didn't sound good. "What else am I supposed to do?" I didn't see any other option.

"I don't know." He placed his hands on my arms and rubbed them. "But we're going to figure this out together.

You're not pushing me away anymore. If you leave, I'll find you. Even if I have to get that freaky witch to help."

"I like the sound of that." Those words had always seemed so scary before now.

"Me too." His eyes fell back to my lips. "Dammit, I really want to kiss you right now."

"What's stopping you?" At that moment, his lips on mine seemed like the most important thing.

"We'd be heading back to that witch for another spell."

"When you put it that way…" I hated the situation we were in. "I don't know what to do."

"For tonight, why don't we go hang out at your place and just be a guy and his girlfriend spending time at her house." He tugged me toward the car. "And then tomorrow, I'll come pick you up for breakfast, and we'll get back to the serious matters at hand."

"Are you trying to seduce me like a human?" Mates usually didn't hold back and typically cemented their bond as soon as possible.

"Oh, hell, no." He tugged me into his arms again and winked. "I'm seducing you as a wolf taking care of his mate. Putting her needs above my own."

"Even though I fought it at first, I'm so damn glad we're finally together." It all seemed so pointless now.

"Let's start over again, no secrets from here on out." He let go of my arm and headed over to the passenger door. "Your chariot awaits."

"For you to be such an alpha, I never expected the word chariot to pass through those lips." He was being exactly what I needed right now. Destiny did have a way of making things work.

"If you tell anyone, I'll be forced to tell them about your secret." He raised an eyebrow and pursed his lips.

My heart felt like it fell to my stomach. "What?" Here I was thinking we might be able to work through everything, and then he threatened me like that.

"Hey." His forehead lined with worry, and he stepped closer, taking my hand. "I was kidding. I was only going to say that I'd tell them you liked me."

Of course. I was being ridiculous. "I'm sorry. It's just that I'm a little on edge."

"No, after what you just told me, I shouldn't have joked about it." He took my hand and led me to the car. "Come on. Let's go and relax."

Everything seemed perfect right then. Not only had I found my mate, but he was being supportive in every way. But for some reason, this added to my hysteria. The other shoe had to drop at some point.

CHAPTER THIRTEEN

The next morning, I woke up with a goofy grin on my face. I glanced at the clock and realized it was only ten minutes until my alarm would go off. The previous night with Mason had been more than I could've ever imagined. He was kind, attentive, and made sure that I was okay before he left. It was hard to believe how we treated each other before then.

I'd told him that we needed to tell my guardians everything we'd learned. Even though I'd messed up, I couldn't keep things from them, especially when I might have inadvertently put them in danger.

It was time to come clean and determine a plan of action. I jumped out of bed and began searching my closet for an outfit to wear. I'd never worried about how I dressed before, but that had all changed. I pulled out a hunter green romper that hit right above my knees and had short, puffy sleeves. I remembered Kassie buying it for me and telling me, "You never know when things like this will come in handy." I'd never thought she'd be right, but here I was, being proved wrong yet again.

Not wasting any more time, I jumped in the shower and quickly washed my hair and bathed. I got out, threw on my outfit, and blew my hair dry. It wasn't long before I was back in my room, sitting at my makeup counter, putting on my makeup. I couldn't remember the last time I'd put so much thought into my appearance.

I opted for a medium pink color for my lips and a neutral brown for my eyeshadow. As soon as I finished, the doorbell rang.

He was a few minutes early, and my heart fluttered. I bounded down the stairs, but Kassie was already at the door, staring at Mason.

"Why are you here so early?" Kassie rubbed her eyes. "Elena's not going to be happy."

Mona stepped from the kitchen into the hallway. "I bet she isn't even..." Her words cut off as she rounded the stairway and saw me. "...awake."

"What?" Kassie turned around and stopped. "Well, okay then. Who are you?" She opened the door the rest of the way, allowing Mason to enter.

"Oh, stop it." I jumped down the rest of the stairs, and Mason reached for me and pulled me into his arms.

"Sorry I'm here early." He whispered into my hair.

"Don't be." I snuggled into him. "I'm glad you're here."

"What the hell is going on?" Kassie's voice was loud but not from anger, more from hysteria. "She's got to be sick."

Mason's chest shook. "At least I know no other guy has picked you up before."

I pushed back and smacked him on the chest. "Behave."

"I'm not sure if I'm happy about this." Kassie's mouth was slightly open as she turned to Mona.

"We told her to make friends." Mona shrugged and glanced back at me. "Obviously, she has."

"Friends, not men." Kassie shook her head and glared at him. "And he's a wolf at that."

"You can't blame her." Mona winked at him. "He's certainly eye-candy."

"Ew. Stop." Yes, he was hot as hell, but I didn't want to hear someone that was essentially my mother say that.

"I've got eyes, and blood runs through these veins." She laughed. "I call 'em like I see them."

"Even though she's tempting as hell, I only have eyes for you." He leaned over and kissed my cheek.

I figured we'd better rein it in before it got too awkward for me. "Do you guys have some time to talk to us?"

"It's Sunday, and neither of us are working, so yeah." Kassie's shoulders tensed, but she nodded her head.

"Let's move this to the kitchen. I need some coffee." Shifter or not, I needed caffeine.

"Sounds like a plan." Mona waved Kassie on.

As the two of them walked away, Mason slid his hand into mine and gently turned me toward him. "I had an idea last night that I want to run past you."

"Let's go into the kitchen and talk about it with them." I nodded my head toward the kitchen door. "I want them to know everything. They deserve it."

"Okay." He nodded his head and followed me into the room.

Mona was at the Keurig machine, making a cup of coffee. "Do you want some?"

"Do I breathe oxygen?" She knew me better than that.

"That wasn't really directed at you." She shook her head and grinned. "I already know your answer, I was asking..."

"Mason." He winked at her. "And if you don't mind, I'd love some."

"So what are your intentions with Elena?" Kassie tapped her finger on the table. "We know nothing about you."

I loved the bluntness of these two women so much. "Well, first off, he's my mate."

"What?" Mona paused and glanced back and forth between him and me. "And you're just telling us now."

"To be honest, we tried to fight it." Now that we were laying it all on the line with my guardians, I couldn't help but feel overcome with guilt.

"Are you serious?" Kassie shook her head and groaned. "That's the worst thing you can do. It forces the bond that way."

"Yeah, we kind of learned that the hard way."

"Why didn't you tell us?" Mona grabbed the two cups of coffee she just made and brought them over to Mason and me. "We could've helped."

"I know, I just…" I glanced toward the window, not sure how to proceed.

"She was trying to protect all of us." Mason sat at the table, bringing our coffees with him, and patted the seat next to him for me to sit. "She doesn't want to worry you two."

"But that's our job." Kassie pointed at herself. "I want to worry so we don't find out weeks later that a vampire is stalking you at work."

"Stalking? Work?" Mason turned his head in my direction and narrowed his eyes. "I thought we were finally on the same page."

"I referenced it at the witch's place." Okay, I wanted to take it back. Doing this was stupid, but there wasn't anything I could do about it now. "One of them keeps showing up at my work."

"Where do you work?" Mason's shoulders tensed.

"The Flying Monkey." I hated the name. "It's just ten minutes from campus."

"Yeah, I know where it is." Mason frowned and crossed his arms. "What do you do there?"

"I work in the kitchen." I sat next to him and placed my hand on his arm. "Mainly wash dishes, but I have to help with serving food when we get busy. That's how he saw me."

"Great, when do you work again?"

"Next weekend." Brad had told me I better have my hot ass back. I figured I could leave that part out of the conversation.

"We made her take this weekend off." Kassie frowned as she picked up her cup of coffee. "Honestly, I'm not thrilled about her going back."

"It's not like it'll matter." Mona sighed as she plopped into the seat between Kassie and Mason. "They know her scent. They can hunt her down."

"Not only that, but one of them was at Mason's ..." Oh, shit. I probably shouldn't tell them that, "...gym last night. He recognized me while Mason was changing out of his sweaty clothes."

The corners of Mason's lips tilted downward. "Yeah, I wish I would've killed the bastard."

"Me too," Kassie grumbled. "But I bet humans are around where you're working out, so that wouldn't go over well."

"In my defense, I still thought she was human too." Mason leaned back in his seat and took my hand. "And I'm worried that she hasn't shifted. That's not normal."

"We've told her the same thing." Mona ran her fingertip

along the rim of her coffee cup. "But we do understand her reasons."

They weren't sure how much he knew. "Last night, he learned everything after he had to take me to the witch's shop."

"You went there again?" Pure rage flamed in Kassie's eyes. "After all this shit with the vampires?"

"They already identified me." The last thing I needed was to be lectured. I was well aware of the risks. They still treated me like a child at times. "So I don't think a few more drops will make that big of a difference."

"I understand you're mad," Mason's tone turned cold, "but don't talk to her like that. You didn't see the state she was in last night."

He reminded me of the Mason I first met at that moment. He was protecting me. "My wolf forced her way to the forefront, and I almost shifted. I'm not ready to face him." I hadn't meant for it to happen, but my voice cracked.

"Don't be so hard on her." Mona dropped her hand back onto the table. "She's had so much thrown her way."

"You're right." Kassie cut her eyes over at Mason. "Both of you."

"I think I might have found a way she can shift, and the king won't know." He turned his body in my direction. "When your dad said he could feel all his people, was it every wolf here or only the alphas?"

"I don't remember." I had been so young it was hard to retain everything.

"It was alphas." Kassie nodded her head in my direction. "He told me the same thing, and that's what you are. You were born to rule as Queen."

"But what if she submitted." Mason squeezed my hand.

"No way. She can't." Kassie slammed her hand on the table. "She's not made for that."

"No, I want to do it." That was the perfect plan. "Would it be to your father?"

"Yeah, or even one of these ladies." He pointed to Mona and Kassie. "As long as you aren't *the* alpha, your uncle would never know."

"And I could be a true shifter after all this time." I glanced over to Mona. "What do you think?"

"Will you be happy?" Her eyes met mine.

"Are you seriously entertaining this idea?" Kassie's mouth dropped. "She wasn't made for that."

"Maybe fate intervened when my parents were killed." It hurt to say all this stuff, but what if it was all true? "Have you thought of that? Maybe Darren was always supposed to be King, and I was supposed to figure out a new way of life for myself."

"You don't really believe that, do you?" Kassie's forehead furrowed, and she leaned toward to me.

That was a fair question. "The thing is none of you are worth losing for the crown. I'd rather submit and be happy instead of always living in fear. I want to be with my mate and not worry that my uncle will appear and take everyone that I love and care about away."

"And this will make you happy?" Mona took a deep breath as she stared at me intently

I glanced at Mason and then them. "Yes, I believe so."

"She'll have to go to your father." Kassie shook her head and bit on her bottom lip. "I can't have her submit to me."

"So, I'm the only one stuck with your grouchy ass?" Mona arched an eyebrow and winked.

"Yeah, our pack will remain small with the two of us." Kassie pointed at her. "But good try."

That was one of the points of contention right after we lost my parents. Neither one of them wanted to be alpha, but eventually, they had to choose since being rogue was taking a toll on them.

"Will your father accept me?" He was my only hope at this point.

"Of course he will." Mason grinned and leaned toward me. "When I told him I found my mate last night, he was so happy. And when he asked if that meant I'd be leaving and I told him I didn't think so, he asked if you'd want to join our pack."

Maybe this could work out after all.

"I told him I would talk to you about it." His voice turned warm. "If you don't like it with my pack, we can go find another one to join together."

If I wasn't already falling for him, I would have at that moment. "That sounds fair." Granted, I'd never want to make him leave his pack. "So how does this work? Submitting?"

"As long as you recognize him as your alpha, you'll be good." He reached out to touch my cheek. "Do not feel pressured to do this. I was only trying to help solve a potential problem. If you don't want to do this, we can cut off this conversation now, and it'll never be mentioned again."

"No, I think it's the best solution." It made sense. "And you two won't feel obligated to watch over me anymore."

"Oh, baby girl." Mona lifted a hand in the air. "This has never been about obligation. We love you as our own child."

"She's right." Kassie rubbed the back of her neck. "We aren't going anywhere, and besides, who else is going to keep you out of trouble?"

"I love you two." My eyes began to burn as I fought back

the tears. "I don't know what I'd ever have done without you."

"Well, stop this right now." Mona pointed her finger at Kassie then me. "This sounds like a goodbye conversation and makes me feel uncomfortable."

"When will your dad be ready to accept me?" I never thought this would've been possible. I figured I'd have to stay human and fight my wolf my entire life. Now, I was going to be able to embrace her and be what my parents were.

"He said to bring you over when you make your decision." Mason leaned his head against mine. "Are you sure? Do you want some time to think about it? This is a huge decision that shouldn't be taken lightly."

"Yes, this gives me the future I never thought I'd be able to have." I could finally be with him and have no worries. "I'm ready now."

"You do need to be careful." Mona took a sip of coffee. "You need to let your wolf out a little to be able to submit to him before you fully shift. Otherwise, you'll be a bleep on Darren's radar."

"That's a good point." Kassie nodded. "Make sure it's in place before completing the transition."

"Got it." I probably wouldn't have thought of that. "Are you ready?" I turned my head in Mason's direction.

"Yeah, we can go now." His green eyes seemed to glow. "We can grab breakfast on the way there."

"Okay, I'll be back later." Even if I committed to this pack, I couldn't leave them high and dry here.

"Good, the four of us need to figure out what we're going to do about the vampire situation." Kassie stood and took in a deep breath. "I'm assuming he won't be going away any time soon," as she gestured to Mason.

"Nope, you'll probably get sick of me." Mason winked at her.

"Don't try to be coy." She shook her finger at him. "But we all know what's going to happen as soon as she shifts."

I wanted to disappear right now. Was she bringing up us completing the mate-bond before we even had breakfast? "Okay, let's get going."

Mason chuckled. "We'll be back soon."

"You just better take care of her." Mona crossed her legs and leaned back in the chair. "Because we know how to kill a wolf and get away with it."

That was the thing about Mona. She was all sweet and nice, but times like these were when she acted just as badass as Kassie.

I hurried over and gave each one a hug and made my way to the front door. I was going to take back my life this morning. Nothing could go wrong unless fate intervened.

CHAPTER FOURTEEN

Mason stopped at a Burger King and got us some croissants on the way to his house. The food sat hard on my stomach, but it was due to my nerves. To be honest, I'd fought my wolf so long I wasn't quite sure what to expect when I allowed her to be unleashed.

"Are you okay?" Mason reached over and placed his hand on my thigh.

The strong electric currents sparked to life and warmed the skin under his palm. "I'm just not quite sure what to expect."

"I promise it's not bad at all." He glanced at me as his forehead lined with worry. "You don't have to do this. I won't be mad or upset or anything."

"No, I want to." There was no hesitation in my mind. "I'm just not sure what to expect. That's all."

"You're sure?" His thumb began massaging my leg.

"Yes, I promise. No hesitation at all." It meant we could be together the way our bond wanted us to be.

"Thank God." His shoulders sagged a little. "I meant

154 JEN L. GREY

what I said, but it'd be nice to be around you and not fight everything inside me."

"I know." I leaned over and kissed his cheek. "I get it."

We were heading in the same direction as the lake from last night. "I take it that you didn't stumble upon the lake."

"Nope. It's only a few miles from the house." He slowed as he turned on a gravel road right before the lake. "As a kid, I hung out there all the time. It was fun for swimming and fishing."

"That sounds fun." I never had those experiences before. For the first few years, I was highly anxious anytime I left the house. "Does your dad know we're coming?"

"Yeah, I just linked him now." He leaned over and adjusted the air conditioning. "He's meeting us at the house."

"Wait. Who all will be present for this?" That part I hadn't considered.

"Oh, no one. It'll just be me and Dad."

"Do you think he'll find this weird?" The closer we got, the more anxious I was.

"I told him that you were out of balance with your wolf somehow and that you needed to find an alpha you could submit to in order for the shift to not be so overwhelming."

I guessed that kind of made sense. "So he just stopped asking questions?"

"Well, I told him that you were my world and I wouldn't ask for his help otherwise." He glanced my way and linked his fingers with mine. "That's when he was sold."

"The last thing I'd want is for your family to get hurt because of me." Was I being selfish doing this?

"Our family is strong, and nothing bad is going to happen." He took my hand in his. "Believe me."

People can't always know things for a fact. I'm sure my parents expected to live until they were old and gray, and look how that turned out for them.

Dammit, I needed to stop thinking negatively. I did believe in energy, so I needed to stay positive.

A small subdivision appeared in front of my eyes. The neighborhood had a craftsman feel to it, and there were at least thirty houses that were spread out to give them lots of space between. Since the neighborhood was in the woods, each house butted up against a section of the trees. That had to make it easier to shift and run. "Wow. This is amazing."

"It's not much, but we do well." Mason released my hand and pointed to the house at a dead end. "That's home."

Their house was only slightly bigger than the others. Its hunter-green siding made it look earthy and inviting. "Your house looks the coziest out of them all."

"That's due to my mother." A small adoring smile filled his face. "She said our house should reflect us, and what better way to signify an alpha than to be the same color as the trees he loves to run through?"

"She sounds amazing." I hated that she was so sick. I wished there was some way I could help.

"Yup, and she's going to love you." He turned right onto a street that led us straight to the house.

It wasn't long before he was pulling into the driveway and turning his car off. "You ready?"

"Let's do this." The longer I waited, the more anxious I was going to be.

"He wants us to meet him around the back." He walked over and placed his hand on the small of my back, leading me to the side of the house. "He doesn't want questions from the members of the pack until after you've shifted and smell like one of us."

That made sense.

When we turned the corner of the house, I couldn't believe what I saw. Their backyard was angled so none of the other pack members could see it, and there were beautiful flowers that surrounded the backyard. A tall man stood in the center, and his eyes were locked on me. "I can see fate has done you well, boy. She is a vision." He nodded his head at me.

Raw power much like Mason's poured from him. He was maybe an inch shorter than Mason, but he was built strong and sturdy. It was easy to tell that he was born to be an alpha.

My wolf growled at his presence. "Thank you."

"Thank you for doing this." Mason nodded at his dad as he nudged me forward. "This means the world to me."

"She's your mate, so that makes her my daughter." He lifted his hand and waved me forward. "Please come. My son has told me of your great struggles."

"Yeah, it's my wolf." I wasn't sure what to say.

"The best thing you can do is allow him to challenge you in a stare and force yourself to lose." Mason followed beside me as I made my way to his dad.

"Force? You make it sound like she's stronger than me." His dad shook his head and grinned.

"Nah, of course I'm not." The last thing I wanted was for his dad to be more suspicious.

"Then, let's do this." He squared himself in front of me and stared right into my eyes.

I held his gaze for a moment, but when I tried to avert my eyes, it was as if I couldn't. I kept his gaze.

"Elena, you need to stop if you want this to work." Mason's voice had an edge of warning to it.

He was right, but damn it, I couldn't look away.

Sweat broke out on his father's forehead. "You are incredibly strong."

Mason took my hand and squeezed.

My wolf growled, ready to dominate. I wasn't sure what to do. *Do you want to be with your mate?*

The wolf paused as she seemed to look at me. *Are you talking to me?* Its voice was filled with rage and hate.

Yes, if you want to be with your mate, we have to back down to this man. Otherwise, my uncle will find us and kill us just like he did my parents. I had to be damn crazy to be talking to my own wolf. It couldn't be natural.

Fine, but only for him, and I can't promise how long I can be submissive. A growl rang in her words. *But for now, I will.*

She pulled back some, and my eyes finally diverted to the ground.

Mason blew out a breath and chuckled. "You scared me there for a minute."

Before I could say anything, my wolf sprang forward, catching me off guard. I fell to the ground as my body began to snap and break in ways that it never had before.

"Elena." Mason cried, but his dad rushed forward and blocked him.

"You weren't kidding when you said she'd never shifted." His dad's brown eyes widened as he watched me.

"Did you think I was lying?" Mason jerked, trying to get around his father, but he wasn't able.

"Well, no." He kept a strong grip on Mason, but he still had his eyes locked on my crumpled body. "But for some reason, I wasn't expecting that."

Auburn fur sprouted along my arms, and my body broke in half, making me stand on all fours. It wasn't necessarily pain I felt running through my body, but it sure didn't feel good either. It oddly reminded me of the one time I received a deep tissue massage. The masseuse's fingers dug into my body, but it somehow gave me a high.

Before long, my vision became more precise. It was as if I was wearing contacts or something. Mason's earthy scent surrounded me, and I let out a loud howl.

"Hey, it's okay." Mason's soothing voice calmed me. It had always felt like my wolf and I were two separate beings. Hell, I'd just talked to it. But now that she was free, our minds converged into one.

The back door slammed shut, and Ella came running outside. "Who the hell is that?"

Her tone caused a growl to escape me.

"Ella, calm down." Her father lifted a hand toward her. "This is the first time she's turned, so you've got to let her adjust."

"But who is it?" Her eyes locked on mine, and l lifted my head, daring her to challenge me. It was hard enough standing down to Mason's dad. There was no way in hell that I'd be able to do that to anyone else.

"It's Elena." Mason took a few steps closer to me, approaching cautiously as though he was a little afraid. "It's okay."

I whimpered. Why would he be scared of me? He was my mate.

"Dammit, you're hurting her feelings." Ella ignored both her dad and Mason and walked directly up to me. She reached out her hand and patted my head. "Hey, I wasn't expecting you to be a wol..." Her hand stilled on my head, and she pivoted toward her brother. "You selfish asshole. You bit her."

"What?" Mason startled and shook his head. "No, no I didn't."

"Then how is this her first time?" Pure rage made her hands clench into fists. "That's not possible."

I needed to shift back before things escalated too much. But I turned my head to find my clothes laying shredded on the ground. Ugh, of course, this would happen in front of his father.

Ella followed my eyes, and she snorted. "Come on." She waved to me to follow her. "Let's go find you something to change into."

Thank God she figured out what the problem was. I trotted after her, and as I entered the house, I heard Mason's dad.

"Are you going to explain to me how a fucking royal who was of age only shifted for the first time today?"

"How did you know?" Mason's voice was barely above a whisper.

"She's an auburn wolf." His dad sighed. "Only those with royal blood have that coat."

This was already going over so well.

Ella was halfway through the house, so I had to catch up. At least I overheard the conversation so I wouldn't be blindsided when I joined them. Maybe this shifting thing wasn't a great idea after all.

"All right." Ella walked to her closet. "Let's see what we've got here."

Her walls were a teal color, which didn't surprise me. She had a bright and blunt personality, and I'd always felt like that's what the color signified. She had a queen bed in the center of the room with coral sheets. Her room was pretty bare like mine, but she had a pink bean bag in the corner with her laptop sitting on the floor beside it.

"What about this?" She pulled out a light blue dress. "I think this would look awesome on you."

I ran across the room and stood next to a blanket. I closed my eyes and pictured me standing as a human. It didn't take long for my body to begin shifting back into my human form.

When my arms straightened out, I grabbed the cover and wrapped it around my body.

"Hey, you were able to shift back easily." She grinned. "I figured I'd have to talk you through it."

"No, my dad told me his trick a long time ago." I'm glad he did since it worked for me. "Can I have something other than a dress?"

"But it'll look good on you." She pouted.

"So I'm going to go around Porky Pigging it?" She wasn't thinking this through.

"What?" She tilted her head and stared at me strangely.

"You know how Porky the Pig has a shirt on and no underwear, pants, nothing?" I needed her brain to comprehend what I was hinting at.

"But this is a dress." She glanced back at it and then me.

"Let me put it more directly." I took a deep breath. "I really don't want to be wearing a dress with no underwear."

"Oh... got it." She looked upward. "You can borrow some of mine."

That was so weird. It was like we'd reached another, more intimate level of friendship. "Really?"

"My God." Ella threw the dress on the bed and placed her hands on her hips. "They're clean. I'm not going to give you used ones."

"Okay, fine." Beggars couldn't be choosers. "May I please borrow some underwear as well?"

"Of course." She cocked her head and overly grinned so it looked cheesy. "But this makes us official best friend status. So do you accept this status?"

"Fine. Just give me the damn underwear, please." She was a pain in the ass.

"Here." She shuffled through some drawers and threw some at me. "This may be a little too big for you."

"I doubt it." I dropped the blanket and quickly put on the outfit she was letting me borrow. It felt so odd wearing a dress. I only wore them for extreme special occasions. "Thank you for doing this."

"Girl, we're besties." Her smile dropped for a minute. "Why didn't you tell me that you were a wolf though?"

"It's a long story." I felt like an ass right now. "Something bad happened, and long story short, I'd been holding my wolf off from me. I wanted to be human."

"No, I get that." She nodded. "Being a supernatural is a lot sometimes. I'm just glad I don't have to keep mine a secret from you any longer."

"Me too." I walked over and wrapped my arms around her. I figured it'd be weird, but it wasn't at all. "Mason only found out last night after the fight."

"Really?" She glanced up at me.

"Yup, my wolf surged forward, and he was there for the ride." I leaned back and gave her a huge smile. "I was going to tell you today, but your dad was waiting for me, and it all happened suddenly."

"So you're part of our pack?" Her eyes appeared to glow.

"Sure am." I tried to smile wide, but I couldn't get what Mason's dad said out of my mind. It was like it was running on repeat. "Do you mind if I go back out there? Mason seemed a little off with my change."

"More like afraid you were going to get hurt." She rolled her eyes. "I'll let you go talk to them for a few minutes to straighten out the pack shit and your announcement, but then you get to hang out with me."

"It's a date." I winked at her. She'd always been so supportive and good to me.

"All right." She waved at me. "Go calm Mason down, and I'll be out there soon."

"Okay." I opened the door and slowly headed down the hall. My heart hammered in my chest. If Mason's dad knew this, it scared me to think about how many others could figure it out as well. And I wondered if his dad would keep my secret or if he'd rat me out to my uncle. All of these questions swirled in my mind.

CHAPTER FIFTEEN

"Hey, I'm so glad..." Mason's words stopped as he took in my appearance. "Holy shit."

"I'm right here, son." His dad shook his head as he grinned.

"Thank you." This was weird, so I decided to take control of the situation. "For helping me."

"I might not have been so willing had I known." He sighed and ran his hand through his dark hair as he glanced at his son. "I'm hoping you didn't know and that it was only a coincidence."

"Well..." Mason started, but I cut him off.

"I hid it from everyone. How did you know?" There was no way in hell that I wanted to cause Mason potential problems with his father.

"Your wolf is auburn." He arched an eyebrow. "Only royal blood results in that color."

Mark that down as something no one bothered to tell me. "Is that common knowledge?" If so, I was screwed.

"That's brand new information to me." Mason reached out and snagged my hand with his.

"Calling it common knowledge would be a stretch, but older wolves like me probably know." He took a step toward me and schooled his expression. "So that means there are only two possibilities concerning what's going on."

"Which are?" My heart thrummed in my chest even though I tried calming it down.

"Either you're a daughter that King Corey hid or you're supposed to be dead." His eyes stayed on my face.

I couldn't believe that he already pegged exactly who I was. "Why couldn't it be K..." I couldn't force my lips to use the title before his name. "Darren?"

"Because he doesn't have the auburn coat."

"But he's the king." Mason's forehead creased. "So why doesn't he?"

"That's what all the alphas have asked for the last twelve years." He searched for something within me. "Destiny has a funny way of making sure the truth gets told eventually."

He had helped me and deserved to know exactly what he stepped in. "Mr. Lockly..."

"It's James to you." His words were soft, and a small smile spread across his face. "You are one of my own now."

To be so easily accepted surprised me. "Okay, James." My heart seemed to thaw a little bit more. "I'm King Corey and Queen Sarafina's daughter."

"You've been alive all these years?" His breath caught as if he hadn't expected to hear the words.

"Yes, I've been in hiding." Now that I started telling the truth, it was just rolling out of me. The second time wasn't quite as difficult as it was with Mason.

As I thought of him, he moved over and took my hand. "If you aren't ready to tell him, we can wait."

"No, it's fine." Hopefully, this would be the last time we had to discuss it.

"Why would you hide?" James shook his head as he glanced toward the woods. "You were meant to rule."

I opened my mouth to say the words, but they were lodged in my throat.

"Darren is the reason why her parents died." The words sounded like they scratched Mason's throat as if it was hard for him to say them.

"Wait." James startled back and sucked in a breath. "When you say he's the reason why, what do you mean."

"He's the one who orchestrated mine and my parents' deaths." My emotions were all over the place. I had never planned on telling anyone, and in the past twenty-four hours, I'd told two people.

"So that's why you struggled when submitting to me." James blew out a long breath and began to pace in front of us. "That's not right. I need to submit to you."

"No." The word was spoken louder than I intended. "We can't." I wouldn't be able to force myself to submit again. I felt it in my blood. In fact, I wanted to challenge him for his spot. "My uncle can't know I'm alive. He'll come finish what he started."

"There's no way in hell I'd let that bastard hurt you." Mason turned and faced me. "If that's what you want..."

"This was a mistake." I should've known and run from here. "I don't want that."

"Then, okay." Mason nodded and stepped closer to me. He placed his finger under my chin, lifting my face so I'd look him in the eye. "We do whatever you want."

"But..." James turned toward me again.

"I lost my family over it." He had to understand. "I don't want to lose anyone else."

The tension thickened between us. I wasn't sure what he was going to do.

"Dad, it's not your decision." Mason wrapped an arm around me and stared his dad down. "It's hers."

"This is my pack." James pointed in the direction where all the other houses resided. "I can't let one person outweigh the others."

Whether I liked it or not, I respected his argument. "You're right. And I unfairly put you in an uncomfortable situation." I wished I'd known all this before now. "Had I known that I had a red coat and what the implications were, I never would have put you in a situation like this. So for that, I'm sorry." I took a step toward him. "Do you want to denounce me, or should I part from you." Maybe if I rushed home, I could talk Kassie into letting me be part of their pack. That was going to be the best bet I had now.

"No, you can't." Mason turned me toward him. "He'll know. That was the whole point of all this."

"What are you two talking about?" James squinted and tilted his head.

"The king can sense every alpha. That's why I asked if you would take her in." Mason's jaw tensed. "I thought you would be willing to help my mate."

"That's not fair." James huffed and shook his head. "I do want to help her."

"Stop fighting with him." He didn't realize how lucky he was. "He's your father. He loves you, but he has to think of the pack, too. I get it."

"You're my pack now too. We'll figure something out." James reached over and grabbed his son's shoulders, lowering his head to look Mason in the eye. "Of course I care about her. She's part of our family now. We just have to be careful."

The word family rang in my ears. I hadn't thought of it that way. It both terrified and excited me. "There's gotta be another way." All this was causing too much drama for me.

"It shocked me." James rubbed his eyes and sighed. "I overreacted, and I do believe you when you said that you had no clue."

"I'd rather no one else know, if possible." I bit my bottom lip as I thought through it. "I mean, other than your wife, that is."

"She doesn't need to know either." James reached for my free hand. "She's got too much other stuff on her mind, and I agree this needs to be kept a secret. No running with the rest of the pack."

"That's fine. She can run with me." Mason's face spread into a huge smile. "We'll stay clear of the others."

"I'm sure you will." James rolled his eyes.

This conversation suddenly turned awkward. "Are you sure? I truly don't want to impose."

"It's fine." He headed toward the back door. "I need to go check on your mother. In a few minutes, would you bring her back there for an introduction?"

"Yeah, sure will." Mason nodded as he watched his dad enter the house.

As soon as the door shut, he turned toward me. "Now, I can kiss you and not worry."

My stomach did flip-flops as he closed the distance between us. "Your family is less than twenty feet away and could come back out at any time."

"So?" His fingertips brushed against my cheek, and my breathing hitched. "I'm not asking for anything more than a kiss."

My eyelids fluttered as his lips descended on mine.

The electricity was somehow stronger than all the other

times. I didn't know how it was possible. His tongue ran across my lips, causing me to gasp.

Taking advantage of my surprise, he slipped his tongue into my mouth, filling my senses with all things Mason. His earthy scent surrounded me, and his mint taste was the best combination I'd ever had.

As I matched his tongue, stroke for stroke, my body plastered against his.

He groaned and lowered his hands, grabbing my ass. "You're killing me."

My hands wrapped around his neck and into his short hair. A low moan escaped me.

"Oh, dear God." Ella's voice was like a cold shower. "No wonder you were worried about wearing a dress."

I jerked away from him and pulled the dress down. I could only hope she made that comment so I would feel awkward. I had to put all my cards into that hand.

"Go away." Mason grabbed my waist, pulling me back into him. "We're busy."

"That is pretty damn obvious." Instead of going away, she finished walking around the side of the house and crossed her arms. "You had her all damn night. It's my turn."

He growled. "No."

"I'm not asking for permission." She tapped her foot on the ground.

"She's not going away." I couldn't keep the giggle out of my voice.

"Shh." He leaned his forehead on mine. "Just ignore her, and she might go away."

"No." She shook her head and moved to stand right next to us. "I won't."

"Ugh." He leaned his head back and groaned.

"What do you want to do?" There was no way we would be able to ignore her. She was determined to get some time in.

"Not sure." She leaned to the side so she could see her brother behind me.

"When he told me you guys were mates, I was ecstatic. Now, I'm not quite sure how I feel since he's trying to keep you all to himself."

"Hey, you had her all to yourself for the first two months of the school year," Mason growled as I turned my body in her direction. "This is my turn."

"You better be careful, Elena." Ella placed a hand on her hip. "He might be peeing on you soon."

"If it kept you away, I might just do it." He wrapped his arms around my waist and placed his head on my shoulder. "Would it work?"

"Nope, I'd just pee over yours." With her free hand, she flipped her hair behind her. "Besides, she loves me more anyway."

"Can't I just love both of you?" I cringed when I uttered the L word. Mason and I hadn't gone there yet.

"You can pretend to." She winked at me. "I won't tell him the truth though."

"She's my mate, not yours." He leaned down and kissed the side of my neck. "So if you want to watch, be my guest."

"Oh, you didn't tell him about that night?" Ella pouted. "I figured you would've told him by now."

"Wait. What happened?" Mason's arms tensed around my waist.

She was messing with him. You'd think he'd know that by now.

"Well, we had a few drinks, and she's hot." She pointed

at me. "I didn't mean for it to happen. It wasn't planned, but we kissed for a little while."

"What?" His hands loosened around my waist. "Are you serious?" Fear shone through his eyes.

"No, she's not serious." I punched him in the arm.

"Ouch." He groaned and shook his head. "Thank God. I don't know how I'd feel if she and I kissed the same girl."

"So you're saying that your feelings would change for me?" Hell, if she was giving him a hard time, I'd join after that comment.

"What? No!" He lifted both hands in the air. "I'm just saying it'd be disturbing."

"I never thought I'd see the day when Mason would care about a girl outside the family." Ella mashed her lips together. "I'm not sure how I feel about it."

"Get used to it."

"Well, what are we waiting for?" Her eyes shone with mirth. "Let's go for that run."

I hadn't considered that she'd want to run with me.

"We can't right now." He dropped his hands from my waist. "Dad wants her to meet Mom."

"That makes sense." She pointed at me. "Tomorrow, I get girl time."

"Deal." As long as it didn't have to involve anything concerning being a wolf.

"Come on. She's going to be ecstatic to meet you." He walked over to the door and opened it. "She'd given up on me settling down."

"Great, so I'm the one who chained you down." That didn't sound great.

"Nope, you're the missing piece that I finally found." His eyes gazed at my lips as I passed by. "I can't wait to get you alone."

His words both thrilled and scared me. If our wolves had anything to do with it, we'd cement the bond tonight. I'd spent my whole life avoiding people, and in a matter of months, I could be committing myself to one person for the rest of my entire life. However long that may be.

This time, I was able to pay attention to the inside of the house. The walls were a light gray with white trim around the edges, and the wood floors were a dark, warm brown. Everything in the house was traditional with a modern flair.

I followed him into the hallway like I had Ella, but we continued past her door and what obviously had to be Mason's. Soon, we came to a door on the left that was partially ajar.

Mason lifted his hand and knocked on the door ever so lightly. "Mom?"

"Come in." A strong female voice answered.

As we walked into the room, I found James helping a beautiful, olive-skinned woman sit up in the bed.

Her hair was long and dark, and her jade eyes, which matched Mason's, landed straight on me. "Oh, you are one lucky man, Mason." A small smile spread across her face as she took me in. "Hi, I'm Dehlia."

"Hey, I'm Elena." This was kind of awkward. I'd never met someone in bed before. "It's very nice to meet you."

"Ah, she has manners." She reached over and patted James's arm with her hand. "Maybe Mason will finally start learning some."

"Mom." Mason huffed but wore an adoring smile on his face. "I have manners, I just don't choose to use them."

"And that's a worse problem." She leaned forward and patted the spot next to her. "Elena, please come sit. I'm sorry that we have to meet this way, but this is all the strength I have."

"It's perfectly fine." I slowly made my way to her and sat on the edge. "I'm honored to meet you."

"I'm just blessed knowing my baby will be taken care of when I'm gone." Her cold fingers touched my arm. "Mason has always been cold and indifferent to others, but I already see warmth coming back into his eyes. Now we just need to get Ella squared away."

"Don't talk like that." Mason's voice turned hard. "You aren't going anywhere. You're going to be here to see your grandbabies toddle around."

"Do you have something to tell us?" James crossed his arms as he looked at his son.

"Stop giving them a hard time." Dehlia waved him off. "You're embarrassing her. Their bond isn't completely formed, so we know there isn't a chance... yet."

His whole family liked messing with one another. "We'll find a way to save you." Even though I'd just met her, I could see such strength and life in her eyes. There had to be a way to save her.

"Oh, dear. It won't happen." She patted my hand again. "It'd take getting the European king on board to allow his healer to help me. All I need to focus on is staying strong for as long as I can."

"Come on." Mason took my hand and tugged me toward the door. "Let's give her some time to rest."

I glanced at his mom one more time. She tried to hide a yawn. If I were Queen, I could help her. Could I allow his mother to die, knowing I could've made the difference?

CHAPTER SIXTEEN

The day had been incredible. We'd spent it with his parents, and I got introduced to the pack. Meredith's surprised expression was worth it when her eyes had landed on me.

Even though I wished the day could last forever, it was time for me to go home.

Mason held my hand as he drove me toward my guardians. "Today was one of the best ones of my life."

"I'm glad. Me too." I hadn't realized how much I was missing out on until now. "Your parents are amazing."

"Yeah, they are." Mason tightened his hands on the steering wheel. "I've got to get another fight in soon. We're going to run out of time."

"What are you going to use the money for?" I'd been wanting to ask for a while, but it never seemed appropriate. After meeting her, I understood his desperation.

"Because if I can offer to fly the healer over, maybe that's all it would take." He kept his eyes on the road and his jaw set. "I've got about two thousand, so I should be getting close."

Usually, when it came to politics, you had to offer something the other person couldn't refuse. I wasn't quite sure that money was the way to go, but I couldn't deprive him of the hope.

When we pulled into my driveway, I noted that Kassie's car was gone. "They must have gone out tonight."

That was one thing they always made sure to do. Go out together so neither of them could get into a bad situation, especially if they were around humans.

My heart wanted to take off when I turned to Mason. "Want to come in?"

He arched his eyebrow and took a deep breath. "Don't ask me if you aren't sure. There won't be any turning back if I go in there."

His words caused a shiver to run through me. I wasn't sure if it was a threat or promise, but either way, my body reacted to his words. "Come on."

"Okay." He turned the car off and climbed out.

Not wanting to waste any more time, I jumped out of the car and headed straight to the door.

It didn't take long for me to unlock and open it. Soon, we both were inside. There was a note on the back of the door telling me they'd be out for a while. My body buzzed with anticipation, so I spun around and planted my lips on his.

"We need to go upstairs." He groaned as I bit his bottom lip.

"Okay." The stairs were right in front of me, so I climbed until we were the same height.

He growled and picked me up, his lips on mine, demanding entrance. I opened my mouth and wrapped my legs around his waist. He stumbled up the stairs as I kissed down his neck and nipped at the base.

"You're going to kill me." He took the first right straight into my room, following my scent.

Once we got into the room, he slammed the door shut and threw me onto the bed.

My skirt lifted so he could see my black lace panties.

I reached over and grabbed his shirt, pulling him down on top of me. The electricity that buzzed between our touching flesh scorched, making me ache for him more.

Moving my hand down to the waist of his pants, I slipped it inside. He was hard and ready, and more need exploded inside me. "I don't know how much longer I can wait."

"I want to make sure you feel good." He growled as his hand slipped under my panties. "I've got to take care of you first."

No human ever uttered words like that to me. "I need you. That's what's going to make me feel better." Every cell in my body craved him.

"We'll get there eventually." His fingers began to rub the perfect spot, making me come unglued.

"Oh, God." I moaned.

His lips descended on me as my body began to quiver. "Now, you're ready." He removed my dress and underwear, so it was my turn to undress him.

As I pulled the shirt from his body, my eyes went straight to his tattoo, and I touched it, tracing the design with my finger.

"That feels so good," he growled.

"I love this." I had no clue why. It was a simple tattoo but one that embraced who he was. I needed to be more like that. Maybe I could now.

Not able to wait any longer, I finished undressing him

and spread my legs, allowing him access. I needed this connection more now than ever before.

Just before he moved, he stopped to stare straight into my eyes. "I love you."

The words were simple and fast, but we were both at the mercy of one another. Bonds were sacred, and even though it helped form the relationship between soulmates faster, we'd still feel the same way without it. "I love you too." I moved my hair to the side, allowing him access to my neck.

"Are you sure?" His voice was low and husky. "This is your last chance."

I moved my hips, causing his tip to enter me ever so slightly. "Yes."

As he slammed into me, he bit down on my neck, claiming me as his own.

Pleasure rocked me as he cemented his bond to me, all in that one moment. As he thrust into me another time, I lifted my head, sinking my teeth into his skin as well.

It wasn't long before we were both climaxing, and something inside me snapped into place. A void I'd never known I had was filled.

You were absolutely perfect. His voice sounded in my head, which almost made me fall onto the floor.

"Are you okay?" He lifted his head, glancing around the room.

"Yeah, but something weird happened." I forced myself to laugh once. "I thought I heard you say I was absolutely perfect in my head."

"You did." He wrapped his arm back around me and pulled me flush against him. *It's our mate bond.*

His words warmed my heart. *So who all can we talk to like this?* It was difficult to realize how little I knew about being a wolf. If that wasn't further proof that I wasn't meant to be Queen, I wouldn't know what else could be.

Only each other in human form. Well, mates can communicate even if we aren't in the same form. It's because our souls were meant to be one. However, when we're in our wolf form, we can talk to anyone else in our pack.

Well, okay then. Finally feeling like I belonged somewhere gave me more comfort than I'd ever imagined it would. This felt right. *Does proximity come into play?*

Not for us. Mason turned to face me and brushed his lips against mine. *But with packs, we can only connect if we're within fifty miles of each other.*

His wolf tattoo caught my eye once more. *I love that you have this.*

You like it that much? A huge grin spread across his face. *I thought it was a little bit of a 'fuck you' since we're supposed to stay hidden.*

What? You thought you'd be ornery? The first few months we ran into each other, we both had been assholes. *I can't believe that.*

You weren't a walk in the park either, love. He booped me on the nose. *We better get up and get dressed, or I'll be taking you for another round, and I'd hate for Kassie and Mona to walk in on that.*

I wanted to protest, but he was right. They were too much like my parents, and I didn't want to share my experience with them. *There's no telling when we can do this again.*

Oh, baby. His lips landed on mine, giving me a long, lingering kiss. *There will be plenty more of this.*

Maybe we could be quiet.

The front door opened downstairs, causing me to groan.

"Come on." Mason slapped my ass. "They're going to want to talk to us."

"Fine." I brushed my lips against his one last time.

"Elena," Kassie yelled from downstairs.

As I stood, I bent to grab Ella's clothes I'd been wearing, but the thought of putting them back on after what her brother and I did kind of grossed me out. Instead, I stepped over to my closet and pulled out a pair of jeans and a comfortable t-shirt.

"You looked hot in that outfit." He groaned as he pulled his jeans back on.

"I don't in this?" He should know better. "The only reason I wore that was because my clothes ripped during the shift. They're your sister's."

"Well, you did look hot in it." He put his shirt on and closed the distance between us. "But you look delectable in this."

"Uh-huh." I stood on my tiptoes and kissed his lips. "Let's get this over with." Taking a deep breath, I opened the door, and we headed down the stairs.

"If we weren't sure if you completed the bond, there isn't any question now." Kassie waved her hand in front of her nose. "Good thing we didn't come home five minutes earlier."

Oh my God.

"Can we not have this conversation?" I couldn't believe she just said that. I glanced at Mason, who had a huge-ass smile on his face.

"They're mates." Mona waved her off. "Don't give them a hard time. I'm just happy Elena finally embraced her wolf. So you're part of his pack now?"

"Yeah, I was able to submit to his father before the change." It had been close though.

"Now if we can get those vampires to leave you alone." Kassie huffed and shook her head. "I still think you should quit your job."

"I wouldn't be opposed to that either." Mason headed over and sat on the other end of the couch from Mona.

"Hey now." This wasn't how this worked. "You're supposed to be on my side."

"I'm on whatever side keeps you safe." He patted the seat next to him. "Vampires are a pain in the ass."

"And easily get obsessive over someone." Mona shook her head. "Remember that time the vampire decided that Serafina was his?"

"That was brutal." Kassie closed her eyes and grimaced. "All the guards' lives were lost."

"It's not like I have the job for fun." I refused to put Mona and Kassie into debt, and my scholarship only covered half the tuition. "I can't risk losing it."

"Why do you need it?" Mason tilted his head to the side.

"She refuses to let us help pay for her tuition," Kassie grumbled and wrinkled her nose in disgust.

"You two have already sacrificed enough for me." They had to start a new life and take care of a child that wasn't their own. "I can't keep letting you give up more and more for me."

"Problem solved." Mason leaned back in the seat again. "I've got it covered."

"What? No." There was no way in hell I was going to let him use any of his money on me. *That money is for your mom.*

I can still fight more. He shrugged his shoulders. *It's no biggie. I'd do anything for you.*

Absolutely not. Yeah, we may be bonded, but that didn't

mean I'd lose control of my life. "I'll find another job, but I'm going to give them at least a two-week notice."

"Fine, but I hang out there while you work." Mason leaned back in the seat and glanced at Mona. "Has she always been this difficult?"

"You have no idea." Mona shook her head as she stared right at me.

"I'm not sure how I feel about this." Within two days, Mason was over there acting like he'd always been a part of my family.

"Oh, stop." Mason patted the seat beside him once more. "You know you love it."

I made my way over to sit between Mona and him, and the four of us watched a movie.

The next few days passed in a blur. Mason had started staying with me at my house, and it surprised me that Mona and Kassie didn't complain.

I didn't push the topic because I wasn't sure I could sleep without him any longer.

As I pulled into the school parking lot, I felt as if I was forgetting something. Mason and I had been riding to school together, but this morning, he had to go grab some more clothes to bring over.

It didn't take long for me to make my way to class, and I found Ella sitting in her normal spot.

"Hey, sis." She beamed as I made my way over to her. "It's been a little strange without my moody brother hanging around."

"Yeah, it sounds silly, but I felt weird driving to school without him."

"Wait." Connor turned to face me. "You're dating her brother?"

Dating wasn't close to what it was. "Yeah."

"But he's a player." Connor shook his head and wrinkled his nose. "And a dick. You deserve someone so much better than that."

"You better watch it, jackass." Ella frowned and pointed at him. "I can kick your ass and make you cry for your mommy."

"See, classless." Connor's nostrils flared. "I had thought she was different, but I guess the apple doesn't fall far from the tree."

This asshole was going down.

"Listen here..."

"Please sit down, Elena." The professor arched an eyebrow at me and pointed at the clock. "You always make a point to leave when the clock strikes nine-fifty, so I should get the floor now."

Even though his words irritated me, he had a point. So I sat down and waited for it all to be over.

RIGHT ON CUE, I stood from my seat and made my way to the door.

The professor nodded, wearing a smirk on his face as I left.

He had enjoyed scolding me. That figured.

"Elena." Connor raced after me and grabbed my arm. "Look, I'm not trying to be an ass. I'm just concerned. Mason isn't good for you."

Ella walked out and narrowed her eyes at Connor but kept moving.

"Thanks for the concern, but it's unwarranted." At every opportunity, it felt like Connor tried to play some sort of angle.

"I've been trying to tell her it's pointless." Meredith sashayed over and flipped her hair. "It's kind of pathetic how you're clinging onto him. I bet by the end of the week, he'll be crawling back into my bed."

"See. That's my point." He pointed at Meredith. "He only uses girls for sex."

"Is that so?" Mason's low, raspy voice filled the hallway. He marched over to me and lowered his lips on mine. *I can't let you go anywhere alone.*

What can I say? I couldn't help the huge grin spreading across my face. "Drama follows me everywhere."

"No, I thought Ella was lying." Meredith's face turned a shade lighter.

"My sister always tells the truth even when we don't want to hear it." Mason then turned to face Connor. "You're a fucking pansy, trying to use the concerned friend angle to get her into your bed."

"Well, it worked at least once." Connor lifted his chin in defiance.

"I was drunk and made a piss-poor decision." He was making it out to be more than it was. "I don't know how many times I've had to reiterate I'm not interested in you."

"You've done it at least fifty times." Ella appeared on my other side. "I've had to listen to it since the first day of class."

Connor swallowed and nodded his head as if he finally got it. Then, he backed away, finally turning around to leave us alone in the hallway.

"And you." I turned to Meredith and straightened my

shoulders. "Stop being a fucking psycho." I stepped closer, challenging her wolf. "He'll never be back in your bed."

"Those are big words, coming from you." A low growl emanated from the back of her throat.

"No, she's right." Mason moved his collar down from his neck so the faint scar of my bite marks were on display. "But good luck finding someone."

Meredith took in a quick breath along with a few steps back.

Mason wrapped his arm around my waist and pulled me against his body. "Let's get out of here."

"Sounds good to me."

Even though life seemed to be going well, all of these little bumps in the road kept popping up. Mason and I would get through all of them, but sometimes ripples happen when something bigger is on the horizon. I wasn't sure if I was ever going to find any peace.

CHAPTER SEVENTEEN

After my last class was over, I found Mason waiting for me outside the classroom. When his eyes landed on me, a huge grin filled his face. "Hey, you."

I hurried over to him and wrapped my arms around his neck. "Hey."

"You ready to head home?" He leaned over and brushed his lips against mine.

"Yeah, but I can't stay long." I pulled my phone out from my pocket. "Brad asked if I could come in tonight. Apparently, one of the kitchen aides quit and he needs me."

"Weren't you supposed to be quitting?" Mason arched his eyebrow and frowned. "I distinctly remember us having a conversation a few days ago."

"I'll turn in my notice tonight." I hated to leave him more stranded than he already was. "That way he has a notice and isn't down two employees at the same time."

"Fine, but I'm going to hang out there." Mason's hand cupped my face and brushed along my cheek. "I'll stay out of the way, but if that vampire comes back, I don't want you dealing with him alone."

I didn't like the thought of being babysat, but if he was in my position, I'd be worried too. "Fine, but this doesn't become a common theme."

"When are you supposed to be there?" He took my backpack and threw it over his shoulder.

"As soon as possible, apparently." I took his hand in mine and we headed toward the parking lot. "So I need to hurry home and change."

"All right. I'll meet you there in a second." He kissed my cheek and ran in the direction of his car.

———

When I reached The Flying Monkey, I felt a chill run down my spine. Something seemed off though I wasn't quite sure why.

"Is everything okay?" Mason rounded the car and narrowed his eyes at me.

"Yeah." I had to be overreacting. "What are you going to do with all your downtime while you wait?"

"Homework." He winked at me as he opened the trunk and took out his backpack. "I figured I'd put my time to good use."

"Look at you." At least he didn't plan on hovering near me and breathing too hard whenever a stranger needed something. "Being all mature and stuff."

"Don't get used to it." He grabbed my hand, and both of us entered the bar.

"Thank God you're here." Brad walked over to me and glanced at Mason. "Who the hell is he?"

"He's my..." Shit. What the hell was I supposed to call him to a human?

"Your?" Brad lifted his eyebrows and turned his head.

"Boyfriend." Mason laughed and held out his left hand. "Sorry, we just recently made it official, and she wasn't quite sure what I'd want her to say. Like I would have a problem with her claiming me like that. I'm damn lucky she's mine."

"Wow. I didn't see that one coming." Brad took a step back and shrugged. "She was always the hostile loner kind."

He didn't paint a pretty picture of me, but I couldn't blame him. That was the air I always tried to give off, so at least, I knew it worked.

"I'm just going to hang out over here if you don't mind." Mason pointed to a corner booth near the backdoors and right next to the kitchen.

"That should be fine." Brad nodded his head. "As long as we don't get busy. It's a Monday night, so it shouldn't be an issue.

"Okay, great." I smiled and tugged his hand toward the kitchen.

When he got to his table, he laid his stuff on one of the empty chairs beside him and leaned over to give me a kiss. "I'll be right here." *I'll let you know if I see anything.*

I nodded and turned toward the kitchen, hoping that I was working the dirty dishes as usual. Even though Ella and Mason had broken through my walls, it didn't mean I wouldn't continue being a loner. I still didn't want to let anyone else into my small circle.

"You'll be on dish duty." Brad pointed over to the sink. "We got behind because Suzy walked out on us yesterday."

"No worries." I headed over to the sink and began working.

It'd been a few hours, and I hadn't heard anything from Mason. *Hey, you still doing okay out there?* I waited for a few seconds with no answer. *Mason?*

I put the dish I'd been cleaning back into the sink and washed my hands. This wasn't like him.

Within seconds, I hurried out of the kitchen and found his backpack and books still at the table. I glanced around the room, but there was no sign of him. *Mason? If this is some kind of joke, it's not funny.*

Going over to his backpack, I dug through, finding his cell phone and car keys. Something had to be wrong.

With shaky hands, I picked up his phone and went to his recent call log. Once I found Ella's number, I hit send.

She picked up on the first ring. "Oh, you finally found some time to call me back? Listen, don't give me the details of why you can't answer. I love Elena too much to think of her in those ways."

"It's me." I wasn't sure how to tell her so I just went with my gut. "Have you talked to or seen Mason in the past few hours?"

"What? No." Ella's voice sounded concerned. "I texted him earlier, and he told me to fuck off. I'd threatened to tell Mom that it wasn't snot she found on his sock a couple of years ago, but he still didn't respond. I was kind of bummed. Mom said she had already figured that out."

"Well, then we have a problem." My stomach roiled, and my breathing increased. "I have no clue where he could be." *Mason.* That time it was more of an internal scream than anything.

"Have you tried to mind link him?" Ella's voice grew a little louder.

"Of course I have." My eyes scanned the restaurant for any kind of sign. "His stuff is still here. Hell, even his car keys. But I can't find him, and he's not responding. He wouldn't try to pull a joke on me, would he?" I'd have been pissed, but right now, I was sure I'd rather be mad than this terrified.

"No, he would never do something like this. Have you looked outside for his car?"

"Not yet." I grabbed his car keys and almost ran through the restaurant in my rush to get outside. His car was still where he'd parked it. "It's still here." A breeze picked up, causing a piece of white paper to flutter that was held in place by his windshield wiper. "There's a note."

"What does it say?" Ella's door swung open, and her footsteps were loud as she hurried somewhere.

With shaky hands, I took hold of the note and read it out loud.

Elena,

You've been a naughty girl. Your uncle has been recently alerted that you are not, in fact, dead. So, we're here to welcome you back to the royal family. Unfortunately, your mate was a little caught off guard at our arrival. If you want him and your two moms to remain intact, you'd better hurry to your house.

Sincerely,

The Grim Reaper

"The royal family is fucking with you? And why did they think you were dead?" Ella seemed to have stopped moving.

"Now isn't the time." I yanked the driver's side door open and jumped into the car. "Get your dad and whomever else we need, and meet me at my house now." I hung up the phone and threw it in the passenger seat as I slammed the door shut. I turned on the engine, punched the gear shift into REVERSE, and the wheels squealed as I pushed the gas pedal down. I shoved the gear shift into DRIVE and stomped the pedal hard.

I couldn't believe that the bastard found me. I did every-thing right. Hell, I had no interest in taking the crown back. I just wanted to live my fucking life with the people I loved. Right now, I couldn't focus on that. I had to prepare for whatever was ahead of me. Regrets would cloud my judgment.

The normal ten-minute drive had been cut down to five. When I pulled up to the house, it looked on the outside as if nothing was out of place. It gave a false sense of security. They were playing with me.

Taking a deep breath, I tapped into my wolf senses. There was no point in hiding them any longer.

From the corner of my eye, I saw the blinds move ever so slightly.

They know I'm here.

Not wanting to show any sign of weakness, I flipped my hair over my shoulder and forced myself to walk at a normal speed up the stairs. If I was hedging bets, I'd guess that the door wasn't locked, so I went with my gut. I grabbed the knob and twisted it, opening the door.

A dark chuckle greeted me as I stepped into the house.

Mason lay unconscious on the floor. Blood trickled down the side of his head, running into his ear.

"Elena, go." Kassie's stern voice was barely distinguish-able since there was some fabric shoved in her mouth and her hands were tied behind her back as she sat at an awkward angle on the couch.

Like hell I would.

Right next to Kassie was Mona. Her blonde hair fell

into her eyes, and the black rings around them contrasted starkly against her blue eyes.

These ladies had to have been tortured. "Isn't it a little pathetic to beat everyone up but me?" My eyes landed on the two tall jackasses who stood in the center of the room.

"Oh, don't worry." The taller one who had chuckled stepped in my direction. A cruel smirk spread across his mouth, stretching a scar that slashed across his cheek. I wasn't quite sure where it started because his long, shaggy hair covered his eyebrows. He was the epitome of a pirate but with the strength of a wolf. "You'll meet a worse fate than them."

"Look at that pretty red hair." The other guy was shorter by an inch but just as intimidating. He had a buzz haircut, and his sharp, angular face reminded me of a vampire. "It reminds me of that former bitch of a queen."

"She had more class in her pinky toe than you could ever muster your entire life." No one got to speak ill of my parents. They were strong, good leaders, putting aside their wants and desires for the best of their people.

"You hit a nerve, Bruce." The taller one laughed. "If she reacted that way about her mom, there's no telling what we could do by just trashing her dad."

"Chad, you can't tell me you want me to speak ill of that spineless, piece-of-shit, King Corey." Bruce bit his bottom lip as he scanned me from top to bottom.

They were trying to rile me up. Dad's face flashed in my head, but I had to hold back my rage. "Oh, I thought that would be Darren since he didn't have the balls to kill my parents himself."

"You will address him as King." Chad's voice was strong and fierce. "Not that you'll get to talk about him much longer. His orders were clear."

"Let me guess. You two are supposed to kill me." I had to keep them talking while giving James and the others time to get here. "I mean, it's kind of obvious and pathetic if you ask me."

"We aren't asking." Bruce emphasized the words and took a step toward me. "Enough talk. Let's kill this bitch and go."

I had to pretend I was weak and helpless. That's what most people would expect of me. However, I was raised by two strong, kick-ass women. "Please, don't." I forced my bottom lip to quiver. I had to make them think that they held all the power. "At least release those three first."

"It's cute that you think you can control this." Bruce tilted his head and gawked at my figure. "Maybe we can have some fun with her first?"

These guys were the worst kind of assholes. There was no telling how many other lowlifes Darren had up his sleeve.

My guardians' words from all the training echoed in my head. 'Always let your captors think they have the advantage. Locate all of their weapons. If they are hidden by a sleeve or pant leg, they'll inadvertently walk a little funny. Alpha males are the most arrogant, so feed it. Allow it to grow until they see you as pathetic and weak. And at the last second, make the fuckers bleed.'

Going with instinct, I took a fighter's stance but made sure I didn't do it perfectly. I let my back hunch over and began to take short breaths as if I was petrified.

"Aw, look." Bruce cackled. "She thinks she can take us."

"Just get it over with." Chad waved him on. "I'm ready to get out of here and back home."

"Looks like playtime is over." He leisurely strolled the

distance between us. He shuffled when he walked, and he pulled out a knife from his belt.

From what I could tell, he had a gun around his right ankle. His pants were looser, and he seemed to favor the left side. Hell, I wasn't quite sure, but that was what I had to go with.

As he lifted his arm with the knife, aiming for my chest, I corrected my stance and punched him right in the face.

The force of the impact and the fact he hadn't expected it made him fall to the ground. Not wasting any time, I kicked him hard in the face, knocking his ass out.

I grabbed the knife out of his hands and searched his right pant leg for the gun.

"What the hell?" Chad's eyes widened, and he stumbled as he pulled his gun out and aimed it right at me. "I can't believe you knocked him out."

Well, this didn't work out the way I'd hoped. "I'm so surprised." I had a feeling my innocent act wasn't going to work a second time. But hey, a girl's got to try.

"Don't try pulling that shit on me." He glanced over at Kassie and Mona and shook his head. "I should've figured they trained you. I saw the little obstacle course back there."

I wasn't sure what to say at this point.

"This is unfortunate, but I guess I'll have to clean up his mess." He kicked his friend who was passed out on the ground.

Car doors shut loudly outside of the house.

Thank God. James and his pack were here.

The door had been left open, which was more of a blessing now than ever.

"Elena." James's strong voice yelled out. "Are you in here?"

Chad looked confused as he glanced at the open door

and back at me. "You stupid bitch." He pointed the gun right at me and pulled the trigger.

My animal side completely kicked in. For the first time ever, I allowed my wolf instincts to guide me. I rolled out of the way in the nick of time. Instead of lodging in my chest, the bullet nicked the side of my arm.

When I rolled onto my back, my eyes darted to his right shoulder, and I launched the knife right into it.

"Ow." His gun dropped as he used his left hand to hold the right arm. "You bitch."

The next minute, James and two men ran into the house and paused in their tracks.

Needing this guy knocked out too, I rushed him and pretended to go for his head.

When he tried to reach out and grab my arm to cut off the impact, I rammed my leg into his family jewels.

He slowly fell to the floor with a loud thud.

"Can you tie these two up?" I turned back to James as I looked at the injury on my arm.

"Yup, sure can." James motioned for the other two to follow him.

Now that we weren't in immediate danger, I ran over to Kassie and Mona and grabbed some scissors from the end table to cut the ropes that bound their hands and legs together.

Once Kassie stood and pulled out the washcloth that had been crammed into her mouth, a huge-ass grin filled her face. "You did great."

"Thanks." Now that they were settled, I ran over, kneeled down, and checked on Mason. His chest was still moving up and down, and his heart rate was steady. *Mason?* Even as I asked the question, I lowered my head and placed my lips on his. They were warm, and after a second, it felt as if he responded.

Elena? His eyes peeled open, and he grinned. "Wait." He sat up and took in the surroundings. "What happened?"

"Your mate kicked their asses." James chuckled as he took in the condition of the two men on the floor. "Take 'em back to our home and kill them."

"No." Now that Mason was awake, my body began to calm, and the adrenaline was wearing off. "If you kill them, Darren will know."

"She's right." Mona nodded and glanced upstairs. "We need to remove their weapons and cell phones and take them somewhere until we can figure out a plan."

"Sounds good." James motioned to the two men who had already bound and gagged the two idiots. "Remove their phones and leave them here." He turned to Mason, his forehead lined with worry. "Are you okay?"

"Got a killer headache. Other than that, I'm fine." His eyes caught sight of the blood trickling down my arm. "But she's not."

"I'm fine." I smiled and looked at the wound again. "The bullet just nicked me. All I need is a bandage until it heals on its own."

"A bullet?" He grabbed my waist and pulled me into his arms. "I'm going to kill them."

"Like we just talked about, let's wait until we figure out our next move." I was going to have to make a choice.

"Here you go." A man in his thirties handed me both mobile devices. "Let's get them out of here before the bald guy wakes up." He leaned down and grabbed Bruce, who was still passed out.

The other guy, who had to be only a few years older than us, grabbed Chad's injured shoulder and led him to the door. At the last second, Chad turned and glared at me one more time.

That's when it hit me. My worst fear had come true. Darren knew about me, and there was no hiding anymore. I either had to step up and be the queen that the wolves deserved or die. I wouldn't be escaping death a second time.

CHAPTER EIGHTEEN

A car screeched into our driveway, causing my adrenaline to pump once more. Maybe they had back up.

"Why the hell did you guys leave me?" Ella shouted the question as her footsteps kept moving toward the house.

When she walked in, her eyes wandered the whole room. "What the fuck happened?"

"Language." James arched an eyebrow at her.

"Shit, sorry Dad." Ella took in the carnage around her. "What happened, really?"

I felt bad. Out of everyone here, she was the one left in the dark. I had planned on telling her, but between finding out and mating with Mason, life had gotten in the way. "There's something I need to tell you."

"No shit." Ella placed her hands on her hips and stared me down. "Spill."

"Now listen here..." James's jaw clenched, and he took a step toward Ella. "The last thing we need is more people involved."

"She should know." Even though I should have respected the wishes of my alpha, I couldn't. Not now. As soon as they linked Mason to me, none of his family members would be safe, and they all deserved to know.

"You decided to join my pack. I make the rules." James's eyes flashed with anger as he swung them my way.

"You're right. I did." But this was bigger than him whether he liked to admit it or not. "But we both know how this may go down. Her not knowing may get her killed."

"Dad, she's right." Mason slowly climbed to his feet and wrapped an arm around me. "The more we know, the better."

"Uh... yeah." Ella passed her dad as if she didn't see him. "And telling me now would be better so I don't throw a temper tantrum."

"There was a specific reason why I tried to keep my distance from you at the beginning." I was glad Mason's arm was wrapped around me right now. I needed all the support I could get. "I'm Elena Hawthrone."

"Yeah, no shit." Ella tilted her head. "I've known that since day one."

"*The* Elena Hawthrone." Mason emphasized the name. "As known in the wolf shifter community."

"You're King Darren's kid?" Ella's forehead wrinkled and she shook her head. "You've got to be shitting me. He wouldn't come and visit us when he was supposed to a few years ago."

As a leader, it was a royal decree from long ago that the person in charge would visit every alpha's pack within a ten-year period of time. In those days, it wasn't too tough to visit them all. People stayed in bigger packs and within a closer proximity to one another. But as America grew and expanded, so did the packs. "How could he not? That's royal doctrine."

"Well, when you're the king, you can change things." Kassie's voice was filled with disgust.

"I'm still trying to understand this." Ella took a step closer to me and stared into my eyes. Something flickered on her face. "Wait no, you're King Corey's daughter. You're the beloved princess that died at age six?"

"Yes, but I'm not actually dead." Great, now I was being socially awkward again.

"Honey, we know that." Mona took a step closer to me and patted my arm.

"So that's what your big secret was?" Ella flinched like I slapped her. "Why didn't you tell me? It seems like they know." she said as she pointed to Mason and her father.

"It hasn't been for long." This was what always scared me. Getting close to someone just to lose them. "Mason learned the night after his fight."

"Fight?" James's eyes flashed to Mason's. "I thought I told you no."

This kept getting better and better. "And your dad found out shortly after. I didn't mean to hurt you. I'd planned on telling you."

"When?" Her hazel eyes became glassy, and she held my stare as though daring me to continue. "When were you going to tell me?"

"As soon as we were alone again." She had to believe me. "I didn't want to do it over the phone."

"And you fought the bond with Mason because of this?" Ella took a deep breath and lifted her chin.

"Yes, see what just happened." I pointed at Mason's head and then to Kassie and Mona. Kassie had cuts on her arms and Mona had two black eyes. Their wrists were raw from where they'd been tied and had tried to get out of their bonds. "I never wanted this to happen." My voice cracked at the end.

"You did nothing wrong." Mason grabbed my other arm and turned me so I faced him. "This is not your fault. You were trying to protect everyone, but you can't keep that burden and expectation on yourself."

"Look what it cost you all?" My fingertips touched where the blood clotted on his head. "I could have lost you."

"No." Mason used his pointer finger and thumb to tilt my head up to look into his eyes. "You will not push me away. I won't allow it."

Even though it was selfish, those were the words I wanted to hear. "It's the only way you all can be safe."

"Baby girl, we aren't going anywhere." Kassie crossed her arms and took a deep breath. "We've offered our entire lives up to keep you safe, and that won't be ending anytime soon."

"But you deserve to have your own life." Didn't they see that I was the reason they were all in danger?

"We're all in." Mona arched an eyebrow. "You need us anyway."

Now that I couldn't argue with. "Mason protect..."

"You are not getting rid of me." He glanced at his dad and sister. "You two head back to the pack. You don't need to get involved any deeper than you already are."

"Like hell, I'm not." Ella took a step toward Mason and growled. "She was my friend first, and I'll be damned if I stand on the sidelines and allow her to get hurt or worse." Her gaze flickered back to me. "As for you, when this is all said and done, we're going to talk and share our deepest darkest secrets with one another. I better not be the last one to know anything else about you."

I couldn't help the damn smile that spread across my face. "That's fine if you go home and stay safe."

"No, you're my best friend." She shook her head and squeezed my free hand. "It's ride or die, bitch."

Mason let go of me as I turned toward her and wrapped my arms around her. "I love you." It'd been years since I muttered those words, but in the last week, I'd said them to two new people.

"Of course you do." She squeezed me tight and pulled back. "I love you too."

"As touching as this is," James said as he turned his attention on my guardians, "I'd like to know how those two guys got into your house."

"It's all on me." Kassie's shoulders slumped, and she sat on the couch. "I let my guard down. It's that simple."

"Don't act like I wasn't a willing participant." Mona touched one of her eyes and winced. "Damn. That hurts."

"We went down to our normal bar. I had an itch I needed scratched." She leaned back in her seat and took a deep breath. "When those two fine wolf shifters walked in and said all the right things. Hell, it's been a long time since I had great sex so..."

"They must have known you hung out there regularly." That was the only thing that made sense. "Who all knows you go there?"

"Everybody in this small town." Mona rolled her eyes and sat next to Kassie. "I was just as guilty as her this time."

"Neither of you should feel bad." It wasn't their fault, despite them beating themselves up over it. "I just don't understand how they knew we were alive and here."

"It happened after you shifted." Mason frowned as he

leaned back against the wall. "But it doesn't make a lick of sense."

"Maybe I got it wrong." Kassie frowned and chewed on her lower lip. "You see, I had a dream the other night where your dad was talking to your mom."

"Like a repressed memory or something?" Mona's brows furrowed.

"Yeah, remember that night I had one too many shots at the party and you covered for my ass?" Kassie picked at her fingers.

"It was right after your mom died." Mona stared at the ceiling. "You had one too many shots, and Corey found you outside Elena's bedroom."

"Well, I..." She took a deep breath and blew it out. "I heard him tell Elena that when she was Queen, she'd feel every wolf in North America."

No, that can't be. "But you said..."

"I know what I said." She raised a finger, asking for a moment. "I stumbled, and he came out to see what was going on. I remember how he looked at me with sadness in his eyes. He knew my mother had died. He asked me if everything was okay. And my drunk ass asked if he felt my mother die."

That was a pain that I understood so well. I had to deal with losing both of my parents. It makes you do irrational things.

"Oh, Kassie." Mona reached over and touched her arm.

"He wrapped me in a tight hug, and when he pulled back, I saw a tear trail down his cheek." Kassie rubbed her face where his tear must have been. "He told me that they could only feel the alphas and that he couldn't believe that another strong, compassionate woman was lost." She blinked her eyes over and over again. "I remember asking him, how could he know that? And his hand squeezed my shoulder. He replied that he knew exactly what kind of woman she had to be to raise someone as brave, strong, and caring as me." Tears rolled down her cheeks as her bottom lip quivered. "I should've remembered what he said to you, but it was only after you already shifted that it came to me."

"It was a secret that no one was supposed to know." Mason placed his hands on my shoulders and began massaging them.

"Shit, I did this to you all." This was what I'd been afraid of all along. Confirmed by one of the most important women in my life. I just assumed I remembered it wrong, but I hadn't. This was all because of me.

"Stop it." Ella smacked my face hard.

My head jerked to the side as the sting caused my eyes to burn.

"I don't give a fuck if you're my sister." Mason's voice dipped dangerously low. "You touch her like that again, and you'll be fighting me."

"She's freaking out." Ella pointed at me. "Can't you tell through your bond?"

"How is slapping going to help her?" Mason's tone was menacingly low.

Ignoring him, she got in my face. "This is not because of you."

I tried to look away, but she grabbed my face and forced it back toward her so my eyes met hers. "Your uncle did this. Not you. Yes, it sucks that your parents died. I can't imagine the hell that you went through, but it's time to stop playing the victim."

"Ella," James muttered as he grabbed the hand she used to hold my face and forced it down.

"No, she needs to hear this." She jerked her hand free

from her father's grasp. "Your uncle doesn't help us. He let packs go hungry and refused to help our ill. Is that okay with you? You can make a difference. This isn't about power. You can make a difference in a way none of us can."

She was right. Maybe I'd been looking at this the wrong way the entire time. If my uncle was not holding up to his end and taking care of his duties and responsibilities, I realized I should challenge him. "But I'm not cut out for it."

"It's in your blood." Mason slid one arm around me and placed his lips close to my ear. "Look." He pointed to both Mona and Kassie and then back at himself. "You saved us. You're strong, both physically and mentally."

"If you hadn't averted your eyes when you did the other day, you would've been over my pack." James chuckled and winked at me. "I'm not kidding."

"The fact that you don't want it makes you the perfect person." Mona reached over and patted Kassie's arm. "You've always been strong, and we've been proud to watch you grow into the woman you are today."

All my life, I was afraid of this moment. The pivotal one where I had to decide whether I would follow the footsteps of my parents and lay claim to what was rightfully mine or reject everyone I loved and run away. And now that it was here, it was blatantly clear what I would choose to do. *Would you be okay being King?*

I'd do anything as long as I'm beside you. His thumb began to rub on my waist.

"Then it sounds like the operation to take back the crown begins tonight." Now we had to figure out what the hell to do.

Kassie sniffed and straightened her shoulders. "All right, let me go grab my board." She stood and passed by Ella and James to go up the stairs.

"What are you doing?" Maybe they hit her in the head or something.

"Ever since I had the dream, I've been preparing." She disappeared at the top of the stairs and a bedroom door opened.

"This isn't unusual." Mona waved her hand at the others. "She's always battle-ready."

"Okay then." Ella laughed and plopped on the couch next to Mona. "So, are you like her moms or something?"

"Ella," James growled her name. "What have we talked about?"

"Dad, give it up." She rolled her eyes and crossed her arms. "I'm almost nineteen. I'm who I am. Embrace it."

I loved that girl. "I think she's pretty fantastic."

"See." She pointed at me. "The future queen is a fan." Her hand dropped, and her nose wrinkled. "Ah, shit. I'm not calling Mason King."

"Oh, yes you will." He chuckled. "And I can't wait for it."

"Let's not get ahead of ourselves." There was no guarantee this was going to work. "We still need a plan."

"Which I have." Kassie's bedroom door shut again, and she came down the stairs, holding a huge chart.

She moved over to the recliner and set it up to lean against the back.

It was an outline of the upper northeast of the United States. She had New York City dotted, the Hamptons, and then some spot near what appeared to be Albany.

"What's this?" I wasn't quite sure where this was heading.

"It's some kind of chart that she made." Ella shook her head. "It must be the stress."

"No, smartass." I couldn't keep the grin completely

hidden. "I mean, I get NYC and Hamptons, but what's the other dot representing?"

"That's where your uncle is hiding." Kassie circled. "I got enough out of dick shit before he revealed his true colors."

"So you knew and didn't tell me?" Mona took the cold tone she reserved for when she was about to throw down.

"No, I didn't know." She held both hands in the air.

Kassie may have been the one who came off gruff and strong, but Mona could probably have kicked her ass if it came down to it.

"He said something about his boss heading to Albany. I was going to ask more, but that's when things went south." She huffed and shook her head. "Anyway, I remember your father talking about a family house that was supposed to be shared between him and Darren, but Darren claimed it for his own after their parents died. He showed me a picture once. It'll take me a minute, but I have a general idea of where it is."

"How long do you think it'll take to figure it out?" Right now, time was not our friend.

"Give me thirty minutes." Kassie walked over to the end table between the recliner and couch and opened the drawer. She pulled out the laptop and opened it up. "I'm pretty sure I remember at least part of the address."

"I'm going to head back to the house and make sure those two are properly taken care of." James strode to the door. "Ella, why don't you come with me?"

"Nope, I'm going with them." She nodded her head in my direction. "They're going to need all the wolf power they can get."

"We need to hit it hard." Kassie glanced at Mona. "Go

buy us tickets for the flight out from here to Albany. We've gotta get there and fast."

It seemed a little too surreal. In less than twenty-four hours, I'd be facing my uncle, and there was no telling what was going to happen.

CHAPTER NINETEEN

I fidgeted as I tried to close my eyes. We'd been up all night and were on the last leg of the flight to Albany. My stomach was upset, and I wasn't quite sure if it was from what we were about to do or being on the airplane. Maybe it was a combination. This was the first time I could remember being on a flight and hopefully would be my last.

"Are you okay?" Mason placed our joined hands in my lap and squeezed them ever so gently.

"Do you really want an answer?" I arched an eyebrow as I took in his rugged sexy face.

"Nothing is going to happen to you. I promise." With his free hand, he reached over and touched my cheek.

"That's the thing. I'm not worried about myself." I'd rather it be me who got hurt than him, Ella, Kassie, or Mona. I hated that they all demanded to come, but what could I do. At the end of the day, it was their choice.

"We just need to focus on one thing at a time." Mason leaned over and brushed his lips against mine.

"Ew." Ella used her arms and pushed Mason and my seats forward. "Stop it."

We both lurched forward, and our heads bumped together.

"Dammit, Ella," Mason growled, causing the people who sat directly across from us to glance our way.

Of course, Ella would make sure to draw other people's attention. "We weren't doing anything."

"Yeah, right." Ella plopped back in her seat and crossed her arms. She glanced across the aisle at Mona and Kassie. "Mason and I should've traded seats. I told you."

"Leave us alone." He lowered his voice and glared at her. "Otherwise, you may not make it off this plane."

"I'm not scared." Ella winked at him. "Elena loves me. She won't let anything happen to me."

It was true, and that hussy knew it. "Doesn't mean I'd be opposed to him breaking an appendage."

"You wouldn't?" Her mouth dropped open, and she lifted her head. "Don't worry. I got a ton of dirt on Mason that he wouldn't want shared."

"Oh, really now?" I turned my attention to Mason. "What kind of stuff is she using for blackmail?"

"There's no telling." He shook his head and rolled his eyes. "She has a memory like an elephant."

"Hey, don't call me fat." Ella leaned back in her chair, making the guy right next to her a little uncomfortable. "Did you hear what he just said?" She looked at the guy whose eyes widened.

"Uh... I'm not very comfortable with getting involved." He swallowed hard, his Adam's apple bobbing. "All three of you are a little intimidating."

"I think I like you." Ella reached over and patted his arm. "Most men would be afraid to say that."

"Uh... thanks, I think." He turned his body in the direction of the aisle, trying his best to turn his back toward her.

"Stop harassing the passengers." Kassie chuckled. "It's not fun when I can't join in the games."

The airplane's speakers dinged, and a voice came over the intercom. "We're approaching Albany International Airport. We will soon begin descending and should be on the ground in about fifteen to twenty minutes. Please put your seatbelts back on, and your seats and tray tables in an upright position." It dinged again, indicating it was now off.

Thank God. I hadn't meant to project it to Mason, but his shoulders shook as he chuckled.

"That bad?" He turned toward me again with a small grin. *I'd have figured you'd be a traveling guru.*

Nope. My parents had died before they had begun taking me on those types of trips. *I'll just be glad when both of my feet are on solid ground.*

The next few minutes seemed to speed up now that we were closing in on Darren. I could only hope that this wasn't the beginning of the end.

———

As WE EXITED THE AIRPORT, we paused at the loading station to wait for Kassie to bring around the Tahoe we had rented. We hadn't brought many clothes, seeing as this was supposed to be a very short trip. However, we hadn't booked a return flight for obvious reasons.

Soon, a black Tahoe stopped in front of us, and the window rolled down, revealing Kassie's smiling face. "Let's get in and go."

"Pop the trunk so we can put our bags in." Mona motioned to the trunk.

"Done," Kassie said as the trunk popped open.

The four of us walked behind with our carry-on bags.

"Holy shit. Good thing we didn't bring a lot of luggage." Ella's nose wrinkled. "For one big ass vehicle, the back seat is damn small."

"Just get in, and let's get going," Kassie growled in the front. "We need to meet my contact in thirty minutes so we can get some essentials."

"Oh, did you forget deodorant or something?" Ella threw her bag in the back and ran to the passenger door. "I'm sure there is a Walmart or something around."

"Sometimes I wonder about you." Mason put both his and my bag in the trunk then took Mona's. "It's like she's not all there or something."

"Hey." Ella turned around in her seat and shot Mason a glare. "I can hear you."

"As if I care." Mason slammed the trunk as Mona climbed up front with Kassie, and Mason crawled into the backseat of the Tahoe. "Move it." He pointed to Ella, motioning toward the back row.

"Nope, not happening." Ella crossed her arms. "After watching you two snuggle and cuddle for the last fourish hours, your ass is sitting in the back."

"No," Mason growled out.

Just let her. We had more important things to worry about than sibling rivalry. *We need to get to the guy, and you know she's stubborn as hell.*

Fine. He moved toward the backseat and almost fell into it. *Only for you. She's shorter than both of us and should be the one back here. Not me.*

I had to squash the smile from appearing on my face.

"Hot damn." Ella pumped her fist in the air. "I hadn't expected that to work."

As soon as I climbed in and shut the door, Kassie gunned the car, squealing out of the airport.

The GPS started talking to her, giving her directions on where to go.

Now that we were back on the ground, some of the anxiety had vanished. Whatever was left had to do with what we were heading toward.

The sun was rising, and colorful pinks, purples, and blues filled the sky. It served as a reminder that in times of pain and suffering, there was still something beautiful you could find in the world.

The thrumming of the engine seemed to soothe me, and my eyes began to get heavy.

"So it's almost daylight. What is the plan?" Ella spoke, startling me from drifting asleep.

"We meet with my contact, and then we find a hotel room." Kassie glanced in the rearview mirror, looking at the three of us in the backseats.

"Yeah, we'll need to go after nightfall." Mona turned toward the back so she was facing us. "And we all need rest." Even though it hadn't been twenty-four hours, her black eyes were already fading back to her natural color. The marks on her wrists were now scabbed over.

One of the perks of being a wolf. Super-fast healing.

"That's a very smart plan." Mason leaned forward so he was closer to me and Ella. "If we tried to do something now, we might not be able to hold them off."

"What kind of security protection are you thinking he's going to have?" Yes, we needed rest but also a game plan.

"I'm expecting it will be light." Kassie turned onto an interstate. "He's not expecting us to know anything about it. He claimed the house right before your father became King, so we've never been here."

"Then how do you know about it?" Ella flipped her long blonde hair over her shoulder.

"King Corey had a few too many drinks one night after a fight with Darren." Kassie shook her head and huffed. "I had to break them up, and as I took King Corey back toward his room, he told me all about it. About how some of his favorite memories were there and where it was located. He shared enough with me so I was able to pinpoint it. He woke up the next morning and didn't remember our conversation, so I didn't bring it up again."

"So Darren won't be expecting us at all." Mona nodded her head. "Queen Serafina wasn't a fan of Darren's either, but since her sister died young, she never wanted to try to dissuade Corey from seeing Darren."

"Why is it Kassie talks more about Corey and you talk more about Serafina?" Ella pursed her lips and tilted her head.

"Because I was the king's personal guard." Kassie's shoulders sagged.

"And I was the queen's." Mona turned around and faced her. "That's how we became so close but also why Kassie tends to know more about this stuff than me. The king was the one who made more of the decisions and things because he was the heir and proved the strongest alpha."

"How did everyone know he was the strongest?" Ella glanced at me.

"Well, according to Dad, the royals have auburn fur." Mason placed his hand on my shoulder. "And Elena does but not Darren. So that's probably how they can tell."

I hoped Kassie was right in case I wound up fighting Darren before it was all said and done.

"You're probably right." Mona nodded her head. "And unlike her father and mother, Elena would be the one making the final decisions and not Mason."

"Ha, who would've thought my tough, strong brother

would turn out as nothing more than arm candy." Ella laughed so hard a tear ran down her face.

"She needs someone like him to support her and be part of the decisions." Mona rolled her eyes. "So he won't be just arm candy."

"Shush, guys." Kassie turned off the road and onto an exit. "We're getting close."

"They can't hear us," Ella said in a loud whisper.

"I'm not talking about my contact." She growled and glanced over her shoulder. "You guys are loud, I'm having trouble hearing the directions."

Ella huffed and crossed her arms.

She doesn't like being told what to do. Mason's deep chuckle popped in my head.

Sounds like someone else I know. I cringed when I remembered a few hours earlier. *I kind of outed you to your dad. I'm sorry.*

It's fine. He already figured out that I knew about you being a royal when I asked him to allow you in the pack. So we'd already addressed that. Mason's fingers touched my shoulder. *And he'll want to talk about the fighting when this is all over and done. He didn't want me to do it when I first mentioned it. Both he and Mom asked me not to. I'm twenty-one, so it's not like he can do much. It'll all be fine.*

I had lost my head earlier and had diarrhea of the mouth for a moment. But he was right; that was stuff we could worry about later.

We were approaching a subdivision full of nice, middle-income housing. As Kassie followed the directions on her phone, we approached a dead end, and she turned in at the last house on the right.

The driveway curved behind the house, so Kassie followed the route. When we turned behind it, it was still dark as the sun hadn't risen very high, and someone was standing next to the backdoor in the shadows.

"Everyone, get out. He's going to want to check us all." Kassie turned the car off and pointed to the right side of the car. "Everybody but me needs to step out slowly on the right side so he can see we're unarmed."

"Are you sure about this?" All her instructions and her demeanor made me nervous. "Is something bad going to happen?"

"No, I wouldn't have brought you here otherwise." She turned toward me as she opened her door. "I just had to cash in a big favor, and they might be suspicious. As long as we are careful and let them get comfortable, we'll be fine.

"Should I keep the gun around my ankle or leave it?" Mona glanced at the guy who was staring us down.

"Leave it here." Kassie took a step out. "Otherwise, if they find it in there, we'll be screwed."

"Okay." She leaned down and pulled out a small gun and placed it underneath her seat. "Let's go."

Ella swung the door open and slowly stepped out with both hands up in the air.

"What the hell?" Kassie waved at Ella. "Put your damn hands down."

"I don't know." The guy stepped partially in the light and grinned. "I kinda like it." He was about my height with short chestnut hair that was spiked in front. His light blue eyes twinkled with mirth.

Considering the way Kassie was acting, I'd thought he'd be a scary man, but he appeared more like someone I'd go to the university with.

"Well, if you like it..." Ella purred.

"Stop." Mason climbed from the backseat and stood next

to me. "We aren't here to flirt or whatever the hell you're doing."

The guy grinned at her and scanned her from top to bottom.

"Chester, we're in a hurry." Kassie pointed at the trunk of the car. "Can we get the guns and get out of here?"

"Sure." He scanned each one of us. "Are any of you armed?"

"No." I just wanted to get in and out and get this whole thing over with.

The others shook their heads too.

"All right, if I find out differently, there will be hell to pay." Chester's features relaxed to indifference as he turned and headed across the driveway to the small place next door.

Instead of heading straight to the door, he waved for us to follow him as we walked around it right up against the woods. "You can take what you can carry."

"Got it." Kassie caught up to him as we approached a small door that was cut into the ground with a lock on it.

It reminded me of the storm cellars you see in the Midwest.

He leaned over and pulled out a key, unlocking it. Then he swung the steel doors open.

I'd expected it to be just a small cold hole in the ground, but it opened up to steel steps leading inside.

"It won't take much longer," Chester said as he began his descent.

"Mona, stay behind them, and I'll take the front with him." Kassie quickly followed after him as Mona waved us forward.

"Do you know this guy?" I had to know what we were getting ourselves into.

"Not really." Mona patted my shoulder. "This is her contact. My contacts are more in the south, but if she trusts him, we should be good."

These two ladies were my world, so if both of them were comfortable, I wasn't one to disagree. "Okay."

Mason took my hand, and we stepped into the underground building right after them with Ella and Mona taking up the rear.

The stairs ended at a metal hallway that had to be at least ten yards long. At the very end was a door that had a computer and a scanner on the outside. Chester walked up to it and punched several buttons fast, which made the scanner buzz toward him. He opened his eyes wide and let it scan over him.

"Access Granted," the computerized voice said as the door clicked and opened.

"Go on inside." Chester motioned us in as he kept the door opened. "Pick out what you think you'll need."

As I passed him, entering the room, his piney scent hit me hard. He was a wolf too.

The room wasn't like anything I expected. It reminded me of some futuristic place. The whole place was made of metal, and there were guns, swords, daggers, bows and arrows, and so much more lining the walls. Every type of weapon had to be here.

"We're going to need some daggers, guns, and maybe bombs." Kassie slowly moved around the place, taking inventory.

"Take all that you need." Chester nodded as he watched us.

Kassie grabbed five daggers, two bombs, a shotgun, and a few pistols. "This should do us. We're going to have to be able to shift too when needed, so we don't want to get loaded down too much."

I sure hoped that she knew what she was doing.

"That makes sense." He nodded.

She divvied out the daggers and grabbed a steel container to put the bombs in. There were cut-outs to hold both of them. She closed and locked it so they wouldn't be jostled. Then, she collected the shotgun and two pistols. "Mona, can you grab the other three?"

"Yup, sure can." Without a moment of hesitation, Mona picked them up and carried them around like it was second nature to her.

"I think we're done here." Kassie nodded at Chester. "Thanks for allowing us to get here on such short notice."

"No worries." Chester waved us ahead of him. "Let's get out of here before the sun gets too bright. I don't want anyone nosey coming around."

"Got it." Kassie looked at me and nodded her head. "Go on and get in the car. Mona and I will be right behind you. The car is unlocked."

Mason took a hold of his sister, who'd been glancing at Chester every few minutes, and tugged her toward the door. "Let's get going. You heard the man."

I had to bite down on my cheek to prevent myself from laughing too hard. Within minutes, we were back in the car and heading toward a hotel.

―――――

MY HEART RACED as we pulled out of the hotel parking lot and headed toward the house where my uncle was staying. We all piled into one room, and I only got an hour or two of sleep. Every time my eyelids closed, my parents showed up in my dreams.

Even when Mason wrapped his arms around me, he still couldn't protect me while my eyes were closed.

Now it was after midnight, and we were heading toward a house that I'd never heard about before yesterday.

"We should be there in twenty minutes." Kassie glanced into the back.

Once again, Ella claimed the seat beside me since Mason would have the plane ride home to sit with me.

Everything is going to be fine. Mason tried to be comforting, but he couldn't make that promise.

I just want this over with. My hope was that as soon as my uncle saw me alive, he'd apologize and let me have the crown, but that was just wishful thinking. I was going to have to kick his ass and maybe even kill him. The question was would I be able to live with myself after that?

I know. Mason's jaw clenched. *I hate the bastard who's made you suffer for all these years.*

That was the weird thing. I didn't hate him. Don't get me wrong, I didn't love him either, but he was nothing to me.

Before I could process it, Kassie turned down a long driveway and immediately pulled the Tahoe to the side. "We can't drive up there without alerting the whole damn place that someone is here."

"We'll have to go on foot." Mona nodded her head. "Let's get the weapons sorted and get our asses in gear."

In less than a minute, we were all out of the car and standing at the trunk.

"Okay, each one of us has two sheaths." She placed a set in my hand and pointed at my ankles. "Put one on each side. The dagger should be on the side with your dominant hand because we need to try to use it versus the gun. Once a gun is shot, it's game over, so put the gun on the other side."

All five of us got situated, and when we each stood up, the tension was thick between us. It was time.

"Let's run." Kassie pointed in the direction of the house. "There will be a small gate we have to scale, but we shouldn't run into too many guards. He's not expecting us to know anything about the house, so he'll have a false sense of security. Just be quiet, and we'll get this show on the road."

I'll be right beside you the whole time. Mason touched my arm and leaned down, brushing his lips on mine.

I love you. I didn't want to say anything more than that. If I kept going on, it'd be a goodbye, and I wasn't going to jinx us before we began moving.

I love you too. He smiled at me.

"So... now probably isn't the time to let you all know I've never shot a gun." Ella popped her lips and took a deep breath.

"I figured as much." Kassie glanced behind her. "So you're going to be stuck with me."

"Well, what about Elena?" Ella pouted like she was going to a party without a friend.

"We've trained her in case this day ever came." Mona winked at me. "She can wield a gun and dagger better than me sometimes."

"Well, okay." Ella bowed down ever so slightly in front of me. "You are officially a badass."

I couldn't hold back the smile. "It's taken you this long to figure it out?"

"Touché." She stood as she shimmied up next to Kassie. "Let's get this show on the road."

At least, she was enthusiastic.

"Let's go." Mona glanced at Mason then me, but her

eyes locked with Ella. "No one says a word from this point on."

This was it. I was doing the one thing I'd always feared would happen. I was trying to reclaim the throne. I just hoped no one else I loved was lost in the process.

CHAPTER TWENTY

I t didn't take us long to approach the gates that Kassie had referenced. They were black metal and at least eight feet high with spikes on top of them. There weren't any lights on outside, so it was easier to sneak over them without being seen.

"Everyone can scale a gate, right?" Kassie turned and looked at Ella.

"Uh... no." She glanced around and spotted a tree that was close to the fence. "But I do know how to climb a tree." She pointed in its direction. "It's close enough I can make it."

"Just don't make any noise," Mona barely whispered. "Once we get in there, we can't talk or someone might hear us."

"But I thought they weren't expecting us." Ella frowned as she stared at the house again.

"They still aren't going to be guardless." Mason grabbed his sister's arm and turned her body toward him. "Maybe you should stay out here and be a scout for us or something."

"What the hell?" Ella frowned. "I was just asking a fucking question. Stop being a prick."

"This isn't a joke." Mason leveled his gaze on her. "Either get your shit together or stay out. I don't want any of us getting killed because you aren't taking it seriously."

Both his sister and I were being put in harm's way and Mason was overreacting.

"I know it's not a fucking joke." Ella yanked her arm out of her brother's grasp. "Don't treat me like some kind of pathetic person."

"We don't have time for this familial bullshit." Kassie pointed at Mason then Ella. "You both get it together or you're going to get us *all* killed."

"Now, let's be quiet and go." Mona glared at all four of us. "The more we stand here and talk, the higher risk we have of being seen."

"She's right." If I was going to be Queen, I'd better get used to leading. "Let's go. Once we scale the fence, we'll rush to the side of the house." I pointed to a dark section between the humongous front side of the house and the garage.

It reminded me of the house in the Hamptons we'd stayed in. It was a huge stone house that had to be at least four stories high, and it had a stone driveway that rounded out from the black asphalt driveway, curving toward the walkway, and then continued the arch back toward the asphalt. It was at least a five-car garage.

"Once we all reach there, our best bet is to go around the back and try to find a window down to the basement." Kassie turned and headed toward the gate.

"All right, there is no time like the present." Mona quickly followed after Kassie.

"Are you two okay?" I butted in before Mason could

make it worse. "We need to work as a team or nothing will get accomplished."

"I'm not the one with a problem." Ella nodded her head and touched my arm. "But let's get moving before we get caught."

How the hell did you do that? Mason's tone was half annoyed and half full of adoration. *If I said something like that, she would've bitten my head off.*

It's all in the delivery. He should know. He and Ella were very similar when it came to others telling them what to do. "Let's go."

I took off toward the gates in a run. I jumped to the halfway mark and grabbed the top of the railing that was flat underneath the spikes before pulling myself up the rest of the way. I balanced on a smooth section and jumped back down to the ground, landing on my feet.

Okay then. Mason took a running start and jumped, reaching about two-thirds up the gate. However, when he grabbed at the top of the gate, one of his hands landed on one of the spikes, causing him to grunt, and when he flipped himself over the top, he landed on his back.

Are you okay? I forced the laughter back.

I'm fine. He slowly stood and glared at me. *Go ahead and laugh.*

I can't. I covered my mouth with my hand. *I gotta stay quiet.*

Ella appeared as she jumped from the tree branch to the ground. She landed in a squat with her hands helping her stay upright. She glanced at her brother and rolled her eyes.

Even without a pack link, I could hear what she was saying internally - '*And he thought I was going to cause the noise.*'

Needing to not spend too much time out in the open, I waved them both on to follow me.

The three of us ran across the yard, heading straight to Kassie and Mona.

When we reached them, Kassie nodded and pointed toward the back of the house. Once we acknowledged her, she took off running, blending in with the dark.

As we reached the back, I noticed that there weren't any partial windows to the basement, so I wasn't quite sure what our plan was.

Kassie took in a deep breath and placed a finger to her lips. She hurried off to the other side of the back yard when a light turned on inside.

If we didn't move, we'd be found. I pointed to the bushes that were at the edge of the house, and the four of us headed in that direction. Luckily, both sides of the house had them, so Kassie managed to hide as soon as the back door opened.

A walkie talkie buzzed to life. "Do you see anything?"

"No, it must've been a squirrel or something." The guy walked outside with no concern at all. "You know this happens at least one time a night. Fucking suburbs."

"I hear you." The guy's voice on the other end of the line was loud enough to hear. "I'll be glad when we can head back to the city. I wish Chad and Bruce would give us a call. It can't be that hard hunting down a stupid teenager."

"Let me just do a quick scan, and I'll head back in." He sighed. "These false alarms are killing my sleep."

"Yeah." The guy talking through the walkie talkie yawned. "You're telling me. All right, I'm heading back to sleep. Let me know if something comes up."

"Next time, it's your turn." The guy grumbled and put the device in his pocket. "Fucking squirrels."

As he took off in the direction where Kassie was hidden, she grabbed his leg, making him fall.

He grunted as he hit the ground and went for the walkie talkie, but Kassie kicked him hard in the face, and his head jerked to the side.

She reached down and took his walkie talkie, putting it in her jeans pocket, and glanced right at us.

Your guardian is a fucking legend. Mason's voice was filled with awe.

Well, you can tell her all about it when this is done. I'd always known these two ladies were badasses.

Mona grabbed my arm and motioned for me to follow.

I took a hold of Mason's and Ella's hands, and we ran to Kassie with Mona following behind us.

Once we were grouped together, Kassie opened the door and glanced both ways. When she confirmed everything was clear, she waved us in to follow after her.

To be honest, I wasn't quite sure what we were going to do. I got that we were going to confront my uncle, but other than that, I didn't know what would happen. I guessed we'd have to just play it by ear. He wasn't going to stop trying to kill me, so something was going to have to give.

The house was dark, which wasn't surprising. It was approaching one in the morning. As we made our way to the front of the house, my heart felt like it leaped into my throat. Houses like these were usually built the same with the stairs right at the front door. Usually, there were two staircases on each side in kind of an arc. If I had money to bet, I was sure that's where we were headed.

I peeked into a large den and found what had to be my twenty-five year old cousin lying on the couch. He had several beer cans thrown on the ground around him and he was watching something on the television. I glanced over at

228 JEN L. GREY

the group and lifted my finger to my lips. We had to make sure we were quiet.

"Jay, is that you?" Richard's voice was slurred from his obvious binge drinking. "Grab me another beer."

He had heard us somehow.

Kassie moved faster, heading toward the front door of the house.

Mason and I stayed back as Mona and Ella quickly crept across the opening.

"Jay?" Richard called out again. He stood, and his eyes met my own through the window. "Holy shit." He began yelling. "She's here. Guards. Guards." He began a drunken shuffle over to grab his phone.

I had to do something. I ran through the front door, across the room, and jumped for his phone. As my hands touched the cool plastic of the device, I prepared for him to land on me or something. But instead of weight, I heard a piercing "Ow."

Richard cried out in pain, and I turned to find Mason putting him in a chokehold. Despite that, my cousin glared at me. "Give me my damn phone now."

Did the idiot think that was actually going to work? "Oh, well, since you told me to." I pretended to hand him the phone with my left hand as I reared my right hand back and punched him square in the jaw.

"You bitch." His words were filled with contempt. "I always hated you."

"The feeling was mutual." Actually, it wasn't, but I'd be damned if I admitted that. At one point, I loved my uncle and his family.

Well, there goes me saving you. Mason tightened his arm around his throat.

Someone had to hear all that commotion. I expected a fire alarm or something to go off at any second.

It was as if they heard my thought because I heard yelling voices coming from upstairs.

We needed to catch up to the others and try to form some kind of plan.

Richard laughed as I glanced in the direction of the front entrance of the house. "You won't be able to win. You'll wish you died with your parents that day."

The sad thing was he didn't realize how often I made that very wish. "Karma's a bitch." I lifted my leg up high and kicked him right in the nuts. "Don't worry. I'll make sure, when I take back the crown, you get what's coming to you."

He groaned, and his face began to turn red from lack of oxygen and the crotch kick. "You bitch."

"I think you already said that." I squatted beside him and looked him straight in the eye. "Next time you call me a name, make sure it's a little more creative." I then punched him right in the face, making him fall over unconscious.

Mason grinned as he let my cousin fall to the ground.

A loud gunshot rang in the air.

The others. I pushed my legs, heading straight into the foyer.

Mason was right behind me.

When everything came into view, I came to a sudden halt.

My uncle stood right in the middle with the gun pressed directly into Kassie's head. Mona was being held by two huge-ass guards to his right, and Ella was being detained by another one on Darren's left. A third guard held a gun to Ella's head.

"Well, look what we have here." Darren's blue eyes

matched my own. The one trait that he and Dad had in common. "I can't believe that you knew about this place. I must have underestimated you."

"Well, it was my grandparents' place." I wasn't going to throw Kassie to the wolves. No pun intended.

"Grandparents?" The guard's brows furrowed in question while holding Mona.

"No, she's messing with us." Darren's eyes glanced over at the guard. "She's some manipulator."

It took a second, but I realized who it was. It was my dad's second guard, who happened to be off the night my uncle executed his plan. Back then, he had solid black hair, a mustache, and was as loyal as they came. The salt and pepper hair threw me off though his presence was still commanding. He and Kassie hated each other. Always in competition for dad's favorite. I had to play this realization the right way.

"It's Elena, Tommy." Kassie's voice was strong despite the gun Darren jammed into her head.

"I don't believe you or Mona much." Tommy's tone was cold. "You always tried to make me look bad."

"Restrain her." Darren nodded at the guard on his other side. "If she makes one damn move, I'll blow Kassie's head off."

Not knowing what else to do, I allowed the guard to come over and restrain my arms.

Stay still. I'm going to knock his ass out. Pure rage was evident in Mason's voice.

Don't. I couldn't lose anyone else that I loved. Not now. *They'll hurt them. Try to stay back. If they don't see you, we might have an advantage.*

Fine, but one wrong move, and it's over.

I had to figure out a way to give us the upper hand.

"He's lying. I'm Elena, the daughter of King Corey and Queen Serafina."

Tommy stared at me as if he was considering it. "You do have her red hair."

"Stop it." Darren spat the words. "It's hair dye. You can't be stupid enough to fall for this. Take her outside and kill her before she causes more grief."

The guard holding me yanked me toward the door, which made me realize that we had to do something now. I had purposefully acted weak for this instance.

Darren opened the door as a sadistic grin spread across his face. "We have to let people know that manipulators won't be tolerated."

Be ready. I'm coming in. Mason ran forward and grabbed the guard's shoulder, yanking him backward.

As the guard stumbled back, I leaned forward, attempting to balance on both feet.

Mason and the guard sparred as I focused on saving Kassie.

"Look at what you forced me to do." Darren's maniacal laugh filled the air as he cocked the gun.

Right before he could pull the trigger, I moved as fast as possible and grabbed the gun from his hand. Just as I was pulling it away, the gun fired, hitting the ceiling right above us.

"Look at what you made me do," Darren growled.

Mona used the distraction to punch Tommy in the gut and bent her knees, throwing him over her body.

"Get her," Darren yelled as he wrapped his arm around Kassie's throat. "She's a manipulator that's gone too far."

As the guard standing next to Ella began moving in my direction, she kicked her leg out, causing him to fall on the ground with a loud thud.

"Someone get her, now!" Darren's face turned red, and suddenly, Kassie reared her head back, head-butting him in the nose.

Blood poured down, and he stumbled back against the front door. "No."

Kassie spun around and punched Darren straight in the mouth. Right when she was about to put him onto the ground, he blocked one of her hits and kicked her in the stomach, making her fall backward.

I rushed over to help Kassie when Mason's voice screamed in my mind. *Look behind you.*

As I turned my body, something yanked on my hair, causing my neck to snap back. One of the guards had moved in from behind and kicked me to the floor.

"Get down on your knees." The guard commanded as he pushed me to the ground. "I hate to do this, but you leave me no choice."

"I'm not lying." I could understand why they wouldn't believe me. They believed for the last twelve years I'd been dead. "I'm the princess." I was trapped, and everyone in the house was busy fighting.

"Take her outside and shoot her like the liar she is." Darren sparred with Kassie despite the blood still flowing down his body.

The guard yanked me into his hold and pushed me through the door.

"If you were who you said, then they would've found you." The guard lifted the gun to my head.

"I'm telling you the truth." I had to say something or I'd be dead within seconds. "The car exploded, and those two women in there were with me and saved me."

"I don't believe you." He cocked his gun and steadied his hand on my head.

A second before he pressed the trigger, Mason ran out of the house and sacked him, making him fall to the ground as the bullet flew past and hit the dirt.

The guard grunted and rolled over, getting ready to fight Mason.

He wasn't going to give up without a fight. Doing the worst thing possible, I grabbed my dagger and charged the guy, stabbing him in the shoulder. I didn't want to kill him but make it so he couldn't fight.

"Shit." He screamed as he clutched his arm, and Mason put him in a chokehold until he passed out.

"They need help back there." We needed to get to my guardians fast.

"Give me a second, and then you come. It'll catch them more off guard." Mason ran toward the front door and pulled out his gun. He hurried into the house, charging where I saw Kassie was now fighting someone other than Darren.

Just thinking his name must have summoned him because Darren came from behind the house and growled as he stared me down. He glanced around and realized that it was just him and me that were conscious. "You were supposed to die that day. I guess I'd better take things into my own hands." He shook his head at the guard on the ground. "You're like a fucking cat. How many times do I have to kill you until you're finally dead?"

"What have I ever done to you?" I was a child, for Christ's sake. What could I've done to make him hate me so much?

"You're a coward like your father. He always wanted to do things for the greater good, not make himself more powerful." His nose wrinkled in disgust, and he shook his head. "I kept trying to show him the error of his ways, but all it did was get me excluded from the spotlight."

"Dad didn't want the spotlight." I remembered so many nights of him complaining that he wanted to take a day off, and then some pack would need help. He always made sure to help his own kind. "He was doing what he thought was right."

"Oh please." Darren's lip curled upward. "You're just as pathetic as him. What's the point of being King if you aren't the most powerful? At least you got to kind of grow up even though I am curious how you avoided me detecting you for so long."

I wasn't about to give him the story. "Let's say I wasn't really thrilled at the prospect of seeing you again."

"At least, that's something we can agree on." The front door opened, causing Darren to turn around.

Tommy came outside. "Your Highness, we need to move."

"Not until I'm done with her." He held the gun at my head, and I did the only thing I knew to do.

I called my wolf forward. My body grew smaller as I shifted, and soon, I was on all fours.

"She is Elena." Tommy's loud whisper filled the air.

"She dyed her wolf." Darren's words fell flat. "Obviously."

"That's why you are black." Tommy looked at him and back at me. "You aren't the king."

"Yes, I am." Darren's eyes lit up with rage. He turned to shoot me as Ella's wolf came running from the side. She crashed into Darren, causing him to fall.

Tommy raced over to try to restrain Darren just as my uncle lifted the gun and aimed for his chest. The loud gunshot rang in my ears as the events appeared to be in slow motion.

The bullet lodged in Tommy's chest and he fell backward onto the ground.

Elena, are you okay?

Yes, he shot the guard. I dug my paws into the ground and jumped, latching my teeth into Darren's arm.

He cried out in pain as he called his own wolf forward.

Ella appeared beside me, and I motioned to the house. *They need more help there.*

Are you sure? She hesitated for a moment.

Yes, I want to be the one who takes my uncle down.

Let me know if you need me. She took off toward the mansion.

I rolled into his body, making him trip and fall hard on the ground.

As he began to stand, I pushed my legs and rammed into his side. He stumbled again as I went for his throat.

He stood on his hind two legs right when I was only an inch away. As he lowered himself down on me, his teeth dug into my shoulder.

A whimper escaped me, but I couldn't let my injury affect me. I rolled on the ground so his body became stuck underneath me. As I stood, I turned around, baring my teeth at him.

This had to end. Blood poured from my wound, permeating the air with a metallic scent. I needed to play up my injury.

Darren chuckled in wolf form as a wicked smirk crossed his face.

I limped, hoping to build his arrogance up.

He howled as he rammed into my side, dragging me

farther away from the house. He wanted me as far away as possible so I couldn't get any help.

I dropped my body, forcing him to roll over on me, and I jumped to my feet once more. I lifted my front paws, ready to jump on him and tear into his throat. This asshole had to die. Prison was too good for him. However, I'd damned well make sure Richard and his mother stayed in the dungeon that had been closed for so long. They didn't deserve the sweet revenge of death.

Are you okay? Mason's frantic voice echoed in my head. *I'm coming out.*

As I lowered my upper body, going straight for Darren's throat, he rolled out of the way, so I landed on grass instead.

He then jumped on top of me. His teeth were only inches from my neck.

I had to move fast or I was going to die. I used all of my strength and pushed myself to stand on my legs, and he dropped to the ground onto his back.

Within seconds, he was back on all four feet. Pure hate shone in his eyes. He crouched down and charged me once more.

I tried dodging him as he came at me from the side, but he anticipated my move. He slammed into me and sunk his teeth deep into my shoulder again. He jerked his neck side to side, trying to tear the muscle so I wouldn't be able to move.

All at once, my training kicked in. Even though it was going to hurt like a bitch, I dropped back using Darren as my cushion which caused his teeth to dig in deeper until all my weight landed on top of him, making the breath rush out of him, and him to retract his teeth.

I turned my head sinking my teeth into his neck as I rolled my body off of his.

He growled as he threw his leg over my head, tightening it around my neck and cutting off my airway. I stumbled back, choking on his blood filling my mouth as I tried to pull in oxygen with little success.

We were both desperate, and I had a feeling this might be a fight to the death. When he moved to face me head-on, I was finally able to pull in a deep breath.

My legs wanted to crumple, so it was by sheer will that I was able to remain standing on all four feet. I had to at least outlive him. Tommy and my guardians wouldn't allow Richard to ascend the throne though there was no telling what would happen. However, any alternative had to be better than Darren or him.

Then, I remembered Kassie's words as they rang in my head. 'It's better to be on the offense than defense. When you're on the offense, you're trying to prevent the attack. When you're on the defense, you're only countering and can miss out on opportunities to exploit their weakness.'

I took a deep breath and rushed Darren. I wasn't sure what the hell I was going to do, but I couldn't stand here waiting for him to get the upper hand. As I put weight on my right leg, it threatened to buckle, and I almost fell, but I pushed through the pain.

As I went hard for his neck for the last time, Darren stood on his hind legs and pushed me, causing me to fall on my back and knocking the breath out of me.

A low chuckle vibrated from Darren's chest as he moved toward me.

No. Mason's growl was deep with anger, but he was too far away to help.

All of a sudden, Darren's body stopped lurching as a bullet hit him in his chest, and he fell straight to the ground.

I turned around to see Tommy lower his gun.

"I'm so sorry." Tommy's voice was rough, and his pain was evident. "I didn't know."

Mason didn't stop until he grabbed my wolf and pulled me right against his chest.

"We need to go in and tell the others to stop." Tommy slowly sat and placed the gun back in the sheath. "When they see your color, they'll know."

If anyone would know the significance of my coat, it would be him.

Please go help Tommy. I licked Mason's face. *He was shot in the chest. He needs medical attention soon.*

Okay. He let me go and headed over to the guard. "Let me give you a hand."

"I'll be okay." He clutched Mason's shoulder as they walked to the door. As soon as we stepped inside, Tommy spoke up.

"Stop!" Tommy's voice rang loud. "Look. She is the princess." He motioned for me to come forward. As I did, the guards' eyes grew large.

There was officially no turning back.

IT HAD BEEN a whirlwind after everyone finally realized I was the princess. The coronation was scheduled to happen next month, so I had time to get situated and ready for my palace life. Thankfully, I was going to be able to bring my tight family of five with me, and a large part of that was being able to save Dehlia. I was in a place where I could actually help her.

Luckily, it was easy for Mason, Ella, and me to drop all our classes for the rest of the semester via the internet. I hated to do it, but my priorities had shifted.

I was back at our house in South Carolina, getting packed up and working out my last day at The Flying Monkey. The shift had gone by quickly, and Mason was sitting with Ella at the same table as last time.

Ella had proclaimed that she needed to be there too since Mason was taken by surprise. It hurt his ego, but it made her feel a lot better about herself.

"Are you two ready to go?" I walked out of the kitchen and grinned at them.

"Yeah, I'm stuffed." Ella rubbed her belly and sighed. "I've got a huge-ass food baby. Maybe me coming wasn't the best idea."

"You demanded it." Mason rolled his eyes. "So stop complaining."

I'd already told Brad goodbye, so I grabbed Mason's hand, and the three of us headed outside.

"I had to be here so your ass didn't get knocked out again." Ella glanced at me. "It was purely my civic duty."

"You two behave…" My words trailed off when I saw a similar white paper folded under my windshield wiper.

"What's wrong?" Ella asked and followed my gaze.

I dropped Mason's hand and hurried over to pull it out. I slowly opened the letter, and my heart nearly stopped beating.

Elena,

Sorry it's been a little while since you've heard from me. I would normally say congratulations are in order, but I'm afraid you won't make it as Queen very long unless you're willing to compromise. Be

```
ready. If we can't work something out, it
won't be pretty.

See you very soon,

Prince Nicholas
```

How had they already found out that I was going to be Queen? It'd only come up a few days ago and with the higher-ranking wolves. The public hadn't been informed. A chill shivered through me, and I scanned the area around us.

"What's wrong?" Mason frowned as he took the note from my hand.

I took a deep breath and pointed at the note. "I think the vampires have just declared war."

The End

ABOUT THE AUTHOR

Jen L. Grey is a *USA Today* Bestselling Author who writes Paranormal Romance, Urban Fantasy, and Fantasy genres.

Jen lives in Tennessee with her husband, two daughters, and three miniature Australian Shepherd. Before she began writing, she was an avid reader and enjoyed being involved in the indie community. Her love for books eventually led her to writing. For more information, please visit her website and sign up for her newsletter.

Check out my future projects at my website. www. jenlgrey.com

The Marked Wolf Trilogy

Moon Kissed

Chosen Wolf

Broken Curse

Wolf Moon Academy

Shadow Mate

Blood Legacy

Rising Fate

The Royal Heir Trilogy

Wolves' Queen

Wolf Unleashed

Wolf's Claim

Bloodshed Academy Trilogy

Year One

Year Two

Year Three

The Half-Breed Prison Duology (Same World As Bloodshed Academy)

Hunted

Cursed

The Artifact Reaper Series

Reaper: The Beginning

Reaper of Earth

Reaper of Wings

Reaper of Flames

Reaper of Water

Stones of Amaria (Shared World)

Kingdom of Storms

Kingdom of Shadows

Kingdom of Ruins

Kingdom of Fire

The Pearson Prophecy

Dawning Ascent

Enlightened Ascent

Reigning Ascent

Stand Alones

Death's Angel

Rising Alpha

Made in the USA
Middletown, DE
19 October 2024

62926771R00146